Brothers, Bullies and Bad Guys

N.D. Richman

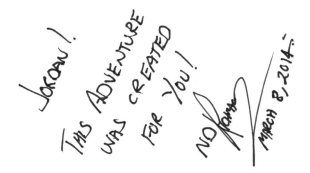

JORDAN !. THIS ADVENTURE WAS CREATED FOR YOU! NO [signature] MARCH 8, 2014

Edited By:
Gloria Singendonk

Cover Design By:
Bespoke Book Covers

www.NDRichman.com

DEDICATION

For Christopher, Michael, Thomas and Katherine.

ACKNOWLEDGMENTS

Special thanks to:
Gloria Singendonk
Hanna Martens
Dara Walker
Linda Spaulding
Jeanette Andersen
Evans Andrews

CHAPTER 1

Chris gripped the grass under him, unsure whether to cower all night or dash for home, for his home scared him as much as the man in the tunnel. He peered over the hedge, across the street and into a playground. The castle beams were splintered, the bridge chains rusty, and the pea gravel overwhelmed with weeds. Inside a storm pipe set on its side to form a tunnel, a cigarette tip glowed, vanished, and glowed.

The man was driving a different car. Parked by the curb, a Cadillac CTS, it was black, or dark blue. As usual, he wore sunglasses, in spite of the dark. They reflected the orange glow of the cigarette, making a bug face when he took a drag. He would be wearing a hoodie. He always did.

Chris shuddered, swept his hair from his eyes, and mumbled, "Crawl or run?" He rose to a sprint position and watched. The orange tip glowed, swung down, and vanished.

"Two blocks," Chris said. He sprang onto the road, blew by the park, and careened onto his street. Within seconds he leaped to the sidewalk, ran over his driveway and, skidding across the step, slammed into his front door. He punched in the five-digit code as fast as his heartbeat and vanished inside.

A floorboard creaked upstairs. Chris swallowed and looked up the stairwell. "Michael?"

Chris scanned the living room. The sofa and chair were colorless and the TV a black window in the wall. The kitchen entrance yawned to his left, between him and the stairs leading to their bedroom. He slunk over and peered inside. Pots and pans, hanging on a rack in the ceiling, chimed against each other.

He bolted upstairs to their bedroom. Slamming the door, he stopped and listened for the noises that often haunted him at night.

As usual, Michael's bed was unmade. Chris crept by it to the window and gazed into the slinking sunset.

The Cadillac roared down the street, its headlights illuminating a bunch of kids, as they scattered.

"Michael and his gang of friends. Wonder who they terrorized tonight?"

Chris threw off his jeans and t-shirt, slid into bed and pulled a pillow over his head. His parents wouldn't get home until after he fell asleep and they'd be gone in the morning. Chris had no idea what they did at the lab; he just knew it was more interesting than him. Since he was eight he'd been left to care for Michael, although he failed at that. He couldn't control Michael. He could barely get him to talk.

"Hi!"

Chris jumped. "Michael?"

"Yeah."

Chris turned on the lamp. Michael stood at the base of his bed. His emerald eyes glowed.

"How'd you get in here?" Chris asked.

"Same way I always do."

"You shouldn't be out so late."

Michael rolled his eyes. "Whatever."

"Thomas? You left him alone?"

Michael grinned.

"He's just a little kid. Why do you?" Chris asked.

Michael looked at his feet. "We didn't actually get him. Got his books though."

"You're such a jerk. You know how important his books are to him."

"Not very. He left them on the road."

Chris clenched his fists. "With your gang of thugs after him? I'd have left them too. He'll pay you back one day, Michael. You'll regret this."

"Get over it, Chris. He's a runt. I'm no more scared of him than I am of you."

Chris glared. "Go to bed." He turned off the light, flopped over, and faced the wall. His legs vibrated with a life of their own.

Michael started muttering.

He's scheming again, Chris thought. He curled into a ball and winced. Two weeks ago Michael put a live gopher snake in their toilet. It clamped onto Chris and, delirious with pain, he fell, slamming his skull into the tile floor. He came to in the hospital with stitches in his head and an ache in his groin so severe it still hurt to think about it.

"Michael?"

"Uh-huh?"

"Why do you come up with this stuff?"

"What stuff?"

"The snake?"

"Uhhh, my other idea was too dangerous?"

Chris sat up. "More dangerous than a gopher snake in a toilet?"

"Gasoline and fire?" Michael rolled under his comforter and faced the wall.

Chris flinched as the truck grill blew into his memory. "Do you remember the truck?"

"Yeah."

When Michael was only five, he got their dad's truck into reverse and backed it across the street. A cement truck swerved to avoid him and plowed into their home, almost demolishing it.

"You almost killed me with that one, too."

Michael sat up and looked over. His head was a dark blob. "Really? How?"

"The cement truck. It came to a stop at the kitchen table, right in front of me. The driver looked so scared I think he just about puked."

"Cool. No one ever told me that."

"I relive it every day."

"Glad I made an impression."

Chris lay back onto his pillow. A car drove up the hill and the headlights swept across the ceiling. "Michael? Are you having someone follow me?"

"Uh, no."

"It's important. Don't lie to me."

Michael's comforter rustled.

"Get over it, Chris, I'm not. Why?"
"Nothing." Chris flopped over and closed his eyes.
"Do you mean the guy in the hoodie?" Michael asked.
Chris' stomach twisted. "Uh, yeah."
"He's been following me, too."

CHAPTER 2

Chris woke with a gasp. His skin prickled and he was sweaty. He glanced at his clock--3:05AM. A noise broke his sleep, but he couldn't remember it.

His mom and dad were talking somewhere on the main floor. Strange. What were they doing down there?

He looked across the room, but his brother was just a shadow. "Michael?"

"Uh-huh."

"Did you hear something?"

"Yeah. Woke me up. A bang or something."

"RUN, CLAIR! RUN!"

Chris bolted upright. "What the hell?" That was his dad yelling. His mom screamed.

"Jeez, Michael, what's going on?"

"NO!" his dad yelled. "Leave her!"

A brawl broke out. Someone was being punched again and again. Men yelled. How many? Five? Six? Something crashed, like the cutlery drawer was thrown onto the floor.

"Get her out of here!" someone yelled.

"What do you want?" his dad yelled.

A man said something.

"No way! You're not taking them!" his dad yelled.

"Get the kids."

The command, not loud, shattered the melee like a gunshot. It pinned the hair on Chris' arms and held him to the bed.

Michael jumped up. "Follow me."

Chris didn't move. "Where?"

Michael streaked across the room and vanished into their walk-in closet.

"They'll find us in there, you idiot!" Chris yelled. "You'll get us killed!"

"Get in here, Chris! Now!"

Light burst from the closet.

"Bonehead!" Chris groaned. He was tired of Michael pushing him around. The closet? Chris ran across the room and plunged in. Michael dropped to his knees and slid to the oak shoe shelves built into the far wall.

"Praying to the shoes? Geez, what the heck are you?"

Michael grabbed the shelves and yanked. They popped open, revealing a black hole just wider than his shoulders. He slid through and vanished.

"Holy," Chris said. He stared at the hole. Where did it lead? How did it get here?

Michael's head appeared. "Quick! Do you want to live?"

Chris tumbled through and dropped. His feet hit a floor, hard yet cushy at the same time. His head vaulted into a solid object, snapping his neck to the side. Stars fired through his eyeballs. He turned and gazed at the entrance, but it spun, throwing him to his knees.

The closet plunged into darkness.

A sound like bomb shrapnel, splinters of wood from their bedroom door, blew into the bedroom walls.

"I want them!" someone yelled.

"No! They're mine!"

Michael swung the secret door closed and latched it without a sound.

It felt like a vacuum sucked light out of the room. Chris heard his heart pound, air escape his tightened lungs, his eyelids open and close, and a bone click as he rotated his wrist. All were too loud!

Deadened sounds penetrated the hideout. Furniture hit the walls. Mattresses thumped onto the floor. Chris grimaced. His Lego Death Star shattered into thirty-eight hundred pieces.

Silence.

Chris released his lungs and listened to the air seep out.

Hangers screeched over brass rails, drawers banged, fingernails scraped over shelves, shoes hit the floor.

Something banged the secret door. It rattled and Chris jumped.

Two pings. Screws?

Michael grunted.

The rattling grew faster. Michael's teeth scrunched.

It stopped. Soft voices faded.

Silence. They must have left.

Chris counted his heartbeats.

He heard a click, and light flooded the hideout.

A tingle spread through Chris' scalp and triggered butterflies in his stomach. His eyes darted from one feature to another. The room spun. Chris felt wrong, as though he had broken into someone's home. Should he even be here?

The room was four feet wide, ten feet long, and twelve feet high. It dropped under the second story floor and into the ceiling below. Black sewer pipes, aluminum heating ducts, and wires flowed through the room and into the attic. A single light bulb cascaded shadows into the walls. A moth fluttered around the bulb and smashed its head into it again, and again, and again.

A thick smell of dust tickled his nose, as though the furnace had kicked in for its first winter run.

Michael grabbed a backpack from the floor, pulled out a laptop computer and sat on a futon against the far wall of the room. He placed the computer on his lap and opened the top, and it slid off his legs and hit the floor. The battery popped out and rolled to Chris.

"Damn!" Michael said. "Give it to me, Chris. Hurry!"

Chris' head felt like it was filled with helium. He reached forward, grabbed the battery and tossed it towards Michael.

He gazed around the room. He had thought monsters lived on the other side of house walls. He sat in their world now. 2x4 studs neatly lined and splintered with nails; the papered backside of drywall, pierced by black screws missing their mark; white electrical wires, stapled to studs and vanishing into aluminum gang boxes.

Michael snapped the battery in and pressed the power button. He grabbed a cable from the floor and plugged it into the laptop. His hands were shaking.

A flat panel TV?" Chris said. "How did you get that in here?"

"I lev…"

"And a laser printer, and a WII? And what are these blue cables?"

"You'll see." Michael threw his arms into the air. "Freakin'! I'm outta power!" He hopped to the floor and crawled under the futon, returning with a power chord. He plugged it into the laptop.

Chris' head started to pound. "Where did this room come from?" He asked.

Michael pressed the power button and his face lit up. "The cement truck. When they rebuilt the house. I noticed they left this spot back here."

"You were only five, Michael. How?"

"You know nothin', Chris."

Chris glanced through the books, set on pinewood shelves built into the wall to his right: *Wiring for Dummies, Visual Basic, Microsoft Server, Snakes and Their Habitats,* plumbing manuals, *Stephen Hawking, A Brief Moment in Time.*

"You read this stuff?"

Michael grabbed a remote and turned on the forty inch TV. "All the time."

Chris scanned the computer programs and DVDs under the books: professional flight simulator, world geography, and financial accounting.

"Financial accounting?" he asked, turning to his right. A pile of taco chips, Crunchie Bars, and cans of Barts Root Beer lay inside a cardboard box.

A grey electrical panel was mounted on the wall beside the door.

"You installed this, too?"

"Yep. Jeez! What's taking this computer so long?"

"Isn't that dangerous? What are the light switches for?" Chris asked, pointing to a bank of switches beside the panel.

"One for this room, one for our closet, one for the bathroom, and one for the kitchen lights."

"You? You made those? The flickering lights, the noises, the voices?"

"Later, Chris." Michael's computer view popped up on the TV. The computer was still booting up.

"I've been living in fear for years." Chris squeezed his fists.

"Chris, I..."

Something thumped and crashed downstairs. His dad yelled, "Get out!"

Michael sighed. "Chris, just shut up okay? I did tons of stuff, but now's not the time."

Michael logged in and clicked a video icon.

"I installed cameras in the office, rec. room, family room, kitchen, our bedroom, and the front and back doors."

"Live Feed?"

"Yep."

"Did you tape me and the snake?"

"No way," Michael said. "It was too dark. Anyway, I wouldn't put a camera in the bathroom."

"Let me guess, you thought it would be unethical."

"Nope. Couldn't stomach the thought of seeing Mom and Dad naked."

"Urrgghhh," Chris groaned.

Their kitchen came into view. Table and chair legs pointed at the ceiling. Empty drawers lay scattered, their contents strewn over the floor. Food, plates, pots, cookie sheets, pans, and utensils were piled into a mountain.

Chris' skin grew prickly and hot. "My God," he whispered. "What's happening? Where's Mom and Dad?"

Michael pointed at the dining room in the monitor. "Is that blood on the floor?"

CHAPTER 3

"What the heck are they doing?" Chris asked, pointing to the office.

Michael gasped. "Look. Guns."

A man sat at the office computer, pounding on the keyboard. Three men stood behind him, holding machine guns and staring into the computer monitor. They all wore blue jeans and green, long-sleeved shirts.

"Chris, our bedroom!"

A fifth man sat at their bedroom computer, just on the other side of the wall. Chris stepped away.

Michael clicked a magnifying glass icon on the computer screen. A single feed view of the office replaced the multiple camera view. Their voices hissed through the TV speakers.

"Will they hear us?" Chris asked.

"You ever heard me back here?"

"Good point."

"Where are we sending them, Kuma?" one of the men asked.

"To the Island," replied another.

Short and stocky, Kuma had black hair, black eyes, and smooth dark skin. Chris guessed he was Hawaiian. Kuma had the aura of one in command. The others kept their distance from him.

"Jet's waiting at the airport. They should land within an hour," Kuma said.

"How long are we staying here?" one of the men asked.

"Till we find the kids, Joe. We need to find out where they came from," Kuma replied.

Joe towered over the other men. He glared at them through steel blue eyes sunk into a face lined with granite and topped with coal black hair and bushy eyebrows.

"Do they think we're alien children from the planet Vulcan?" Michael asked. His lip trembled and he bit down on it.

A man walked into the office. "What are we doing with the kids?" he asked.

Michael jabbed his finger into the monitor. "That's him! He's wearing the hoodie. The hoodie guy!"

Chris' skin prickled. He rubbed his arms. "Sith, so he was watching us."

Michael looked at him and raised his eyebrows. "You call him Sith?"

"Yeah. Kind of looks like Darth Maul, doesn't he?"

Michael moved closer to the monitor. "Gee, I never thought about that. He does."

"That's the fun part, Bill," Kuma said. "We'll torture them in front of Claire and Geoff till we get the information. Then, we'll kill 'em all."

"Why bother with the info if we're doing away with them?" Bill asked.

"It would be nice to know we're killing them for a reason," Kuma said. He grinned.

"What if we can't find the kids?" Joe asked.

"Snot-nosed kids? We'll find them. Either way, we'll eliminate their parents in two weeks. Nobody'll know what happened to them."

Chris' legs gave and he dropped to the floor. He felt hollow, like a pumpkin with its insides scraped out.

"They're going to kill Mom and Dad. Why? What did we do?"

"Dunno. Two weeks. We've got two weeks to find out." Michael's hands turned white and started shaking.

"Found anything on that computer, Pete?" Kuma asked.

Pete looked oriental. Brown eyes and black hair blended into smooth skin and a small featured face. "No."

"Any other computers in the house?"

"Ing, check out the one in the kids' room."

Kuma turned to the door. "Well, keep it up. I'm gonna find something to eat."

Michel glanced at Chris. "I connected all the computers in this house through a wireless network. Let's start with Ing."

From the back, Ing looked like Pete. His fingers brushed over the keyboard. His neck crooked forward, almost pushing his nose into the screen.

Michael pulled up a text input screen, typed, "How's it coming?" and pressed enter. His hands were shaking.

Ing stopped typing and looked above him.

Michael's screen flashed. "Fine. Who is this?" it asked.

Michael looked wide-eyed at Chris. "Crap. How do you spell Kuma?"

Chris' stomach fluttered. "I...I don't know! Hurry up. He's gonna get suspicious. Just like it sounds."

Michael mumbled as he typed. C-u-m-a. "Do you even know what you're looking for?" and pressed enter.

Chris held his breath. The computer beeped. "Yes."

Michael grinned. He typed, "What?"

"Info on the kids. Who their parents are. Where they were born."

"Why?" Michael typed.

Ing looked behind him. He typed, "Don't know."

"Shoot!" Chris said. "That's no help."

"Amazing," Michael typed. "Get off the computer, dig a hole in the back yard up to your head. Don't stop till you're finished."

Ing padded from the room. He slunk past the back door camera and into the yard.

Chris sat on the futon and leaned into the wall. "I don't get it. They know who our parents are. What the heck are they talking about?"

"Dunno, but we're going to find out."

Michael punched a few keys. "I'm backing up Mom and Dad's hard drive."

A blue percent indicator grew on the monitor.

Michael's fingers flew over the keyboard.

"Shoot," Michael said, "they cut the house lines. I can't connect."

"To the Internet?"

"Yeah."

"Geez, Michael. You're only twelve and you suck and school, but you're a flippin' genius. How long have you...?"

Michael turned and looked at Chris. "Been this smart?"

12

"Yeah."

Michael's eyes seemed to dance. "Compared to you, I've always been brilliant."

"Yeah. You've always been a jerk, too," Chris whispered. "Why did you keep it hidden?"

Michael shrugged. "Dunno. I keep everything hidden."

Chris sat up. "There's more?"

"Uh-huh."

Chris watched the indicator crawl across the screen. His eyelids drooped. The computer fan buzzed in waves. His eyes closed and he was falling. Suddenly he was in his school, walking down the hall. The polished tiles felt cool under his feet. Why was he naked? Kids surrounded him and pointed. They dropped to the floor and rolled with laughter. He ran for the gym. He burst through a metal door and slammed it on the crowd, ran to the bleachers, and crawled underneath. He whimpered as the door opened and the gym filled with kids. Michael stood on stage, wearing the school principal's blue suit. He bellowed into a microphone, "We have an award to present to Chris Boulton."

"Done!" Michael yelped.

Chris popped back. The indicator showed 100%.

"Hard drive's imaged," Michael said. "Now." He typed a command. "I'm wiping out the drive on Mom and Dad's computer."

Pete jumped out of his chair and started yelling. He hit the keyboard. It flipped off the table and crashed onto the floor. He turned and dashed to the door, stopped, and dove under the desk. He crawled out holding a power cord.

Michael frowned. "Shoot. I hope I corrupted it before he pulled the cord."

Chris got up and walked to the other end of the room. What did Mom and Dad do? Could it be the research centre? He wished he'd gotten inside instead of staring through the bars. What went on in there? He assumed they designed earth-ending weapons for the military, or something.

Joe stood on the living room sofa, slicing it open with a hunting knife. The knife looked big, even in his hands.

"Whadya think they're looking for?" Chris asked.

"Michael?"

Chris glanced at the cot to find Michael sprawled on his back, sleeping. Chris shook his head. Although built like a tank, Michael's shaggy blond hair and freckles gave him a comical look. He didn't look like a genius, and he sure didn't look mean. Chris had no idea how many kids took a beating from Michael, but there were lots. Thomas, the runt of the school, a kid in grade five, was his favorite.

Chris wiped a tear off his cheek and lowered his head, ducking behind his long, black hair, his comfort zone. He was three when Michael was born but still remembered how proud he was. It was disappointing.

He heard Kuma yelling, "I don't care if you have to tear this house apart. Find the little brats. And what's Pete doing outside digging a hole?"

CHAPTER 4

Chris woke with a jump. He stretched his right arm, then his left. It would be a crummy day. He had a math test which was bad. But it was the last day of summer school, yay!

Where were his slippers? And why was he on the floor?

The nightmare seemed so real. He looked across the room to check his brother but looked into a TV instead. No! The dream wasn't real.

Was it?

He closed his eyes.

"This is a dream."

Something ticked like raindrops falling onto glass.

"Huh?"

His heart pounded, forcing waves, an ebb and flow of blood, into his fingers, toes, and lungs. They tingled. He popped open his eyes and saw a shadow. It fluttered over the wood studs, the drywall, the book case, the TV. He looked up to the ceiling. The moth, the moth from his dream continued its pointless charge into the light bulb. Reality wrapped around his throat and tightened. He breathed with short gasps.

"Jeez, I woke into a nightmare."

Grief tugged his gut and twisted it into a knot. His back muscles cramped. He grimaced and wiped tears from his cheeks.

"No!" he said.

He concentrated on the panic, trying to push it away.

Ten minutes had passed. Sure he wouldn't cry, he grabbed

Michael's shoulder and shook him.

Michael jumped and grabbed Chris' throat. Chris ducked as Michael's fist winged his nose.

"Ouch! Michael! It's me!"

"Sorry, uh, I owed you one, didn't I? Uh, what time is it?"

"Six in the morning, I think. I'm surprised they didn't find us," Chris said. He wiped his nose. "Look, ya goof. I'm bleeding. You punch me one more time, I'll poke your eyes out."

Michael grabbed a box of Kleenex. "Here."

"Man, that hurts," Chris said.

Michael patted his stomach. "I'm hungry."

"Whatta ya got?"

Michael pulled a box from under the futon. "Chips and pop."

"Sounds good."

Michael tossed Chris a root beer and split open a bag of cheese nachos.

"We've gotta get out of here," Chris said through a mouthful of chips, "somewhere safe."

Michael flopped onto the futon. "Where?"

"I'm thinking." Chris swallowed and chugged some root beer. "Where's your cell phone?"

"On the pad."

Chris glanced at the floor. The charge pad was almost right underneath them. "Darn. I don't know where mine is."

"Chris?" Michael's eyes bulged.

"Mmmhhmmm?"

"I gotta go."

Chris stopped chewing. "Bathroom?"

"Uh-huh."

"Oh." Chris swallowed and guzzled some root beer. "Use the waste line. The one you diverted from the bathtub drain."

"No way. That's a one inch line. I'm way beyond that." Michael stood up and bounced on his toes.

"Do you have a blender? We can whip it up and pour it down."

Michael kicked the bag of chips out of Chris' hand, sending a plume of nachos into the air. "You're gross!"

"Smooth, Michael. Real smooth. How about a spoon then?"

Michael grabbed his pocketknife from the bookshelf and waved it in Chris' face. "Look, Mom and Dad's bathroom. I'll crawl over the ceiling tiles and cut a hole through the drywall."

Chris looked at the wall to his left. It extended below the floor into a dead space underneath the entire top floor of the house, including the bathroom, the movie room, the office, and his parents' room located across the hall opposite their bedroom. The bottom of the dead space was the main floor ceiling, covering the kitchen, living, dining, and laundry rooms. A matrix of steel hangers attached to metal joists and hung at two foot intervals supported the suspended ceiling from the floor above. There was a wall about forty feet away. "You're sure that's the bathroom? And what if they find the hole you cut?"

"I'm sure. The cupboard's on the other side. I'll hide the hole with towels."

"But, what if someone's in there?"

Michael crouched beside Chris. "I'll crawl there and wait. You watch through the hallway camera. I'll cut the hole, crawl through, and lock the door. Simple."

Chris felt his face flush. "What if they hear you, Michael? What if someone walks in while you're crawling through the cupboard?"

"What if I crap my pants and you have to smell it for the next eight hours?"

Chris stood up and sighed. "Fine…don't blame me if you get killed."

"I'll be dead. Come on. Help me."

Michael poked his knife through the plastic and sliced it open.

"What's the plastic for anyway?"

Michael crawled through and squeezed between two vertical studs. "Sound barrier."

He bear walked onto the steel trusses, laid parallel across the ceiling, two feet apart. Only his hands and feet touched the trusses, like a permanent push up.

Chris leaned into the dead space and glanced at the ceiling tiles. Kuma's gang talked somewhere beneath them. This was stupid. Something would go wrong. It had to.

Michael had crawled over five beams. His arms and legs shook. His bum dropped and weaved.

"Come on, Michael. You can do it!" Chris whispered.

Michael lunged for the next truss, pulled up his leg, and farted like a bagpipe. Chris started to laugh, then clapped his hands over his mouth and ran to the monitor. Kuma and his gang stared at the ceiling, then at each other. "Ventriloquist farter?" Kuma asked. He smiled and they laughed.

Kuma raised his machine gun and prodded the ceiling tile.

The tile under Michael's knees jumped.

Chris parted the plastic and waved Michael on. He whispered, "Keep going."

Michael stretched out and grabbed the next beam. He pulled his right leg up and slipped. His foot crashed into the ceiling tile.

Chris wrapped his arms around his stomach. "No!"

Michael coiled his body and threw himself onto the ceiling below.

CHAPTER 5

The world started to robot dance. Chunks of tile fluttered as though caught in a strobe light. Michael's knife floated from his hand, flipped and paused, showing the nick in the handle, and flipped and paused. Michael fell through the ceiling.

Chris ran to the monitor. He heard a sickening crack as Michael landed on Ing's head. A machine gun jumped out of Ing's hands and into Michael's.

Michael pulled the trigger.

"Phuh!"

Recoil knocked Michael to the hardwood floor and spun him like a top. Bullets sprayed from his gun. The TV screen blew out like a square chunk of Jello, spewing electronic components into a cloud. The couch exploded into white fluff. Vases, windows, and picture frames showered the room with glass.

Bill popped up from behind the couch, pointed his gun at Michael, and pulled the trigger.

Chris hopped up and down. "Hurry!"

Michael tossed the gun and ran up the stairs as the wall beside him shattered into wood splinters and dust.

Chris threw open the hideout door. Michael careened into the closet. Pants and shirts flew through the opening. A running shoe smacked Chris' face.

"Ouch!"

Michael dove in and Chris slammed the door. Michael was white, his eyes red, and he smelled bad. "We're dead! We're dead! We're dead!"

Chris grabbed him. "Michael! Stop! We have to get out of here!"

"But…"

"Think! What do we need?"

"Laptop, memory stick, g…gidgit bag."

"Gidgit bag?"

"Gadgets, tools, s…software. It's under the bed."

"Did they see where you went?" Chris asked.

"Don't think so."

"Good. Get changed. You stink." Chris grabbed Michael's jeans and threw them at him.

"I'll pack the laptop," Chris said.

Chris jumped into his jeans, T-shirt, socks, and high-tops, grabbed the laptop, and stuffed it into a leather carrying case. He reached under the bed and retrieved the gidgit bag, a nylon backpack. Michael was dressed and holding a package of diaper wipes in one hand and a full ice cream bucket in the other. His skin white and his knees bent too far, he swayed like he was about to collapse.

"Do you know where the truck keys are?" Chris asked.

Michael placed the bucket and wipes on the floor and reached into his jeans pocket. "Right here."

"Where did you get those? No, forget it. I don't want to know. Can we divert them? What about the spook system?"

"Spook system?"

Chris pointed to the monitor. "Yeah. The one you used to scare the hell out of me."

"Oh, that one," Michael said. He grabbed the gidget bag from Chris. "Give me the laptop. I can turn on the TV. If they run to the movie room we can sneak out behind them."

Michael opened the laptop and pressed the power button. "You ready?"

Something thumped in the closet. "Hurry. I think they're in our bedroom."

Michael's fingers blurred over the keyboard. The upstairs TV turned on and a familiar tune burst through the house.

"Jeopardy. How appropriate," Chris mumbled.

"Heh. A little Freddy chainsaw for added confusion," Michael said. He typed in a command. The sound of a chainsaw burst over the house sound system.

Chris pushed open the shoe shelves and peeked into the closet. It was empty. He crawled out and dashed to the bedroom door. Only half the door remained, the rest laying on the floor in shards. He squeezed behind it and peeked into the hallway. Michael pressed into his back. Kuma and his men thundered by like a herd of giant sheep.

"Careful!" Joe said as he dashed by. "The brats have a chain saw."

"I hope they're all in there," Chris whispered. He stepped into the hallway and tip-toed down the stairs, around chunks of drywall, wood splinters, nails, and screws. He ducked and crawled under the landing wall.

"That wall was supposed to be me," Michael said.

Kuma's voice grew behind them. "Hurry, they're coming," Chris whispered. He gripped the garage door and pulled it open. It squealed.

"Run, Michael."

"But my phone. It's in the kitchen."

"No time."

Chris dashed to the truck.

Michael slammed the door so hard a can of nails popped off the shelf and crashed onto the floor. "Doh!"

Chris threw up his hands. "Michael!"

Chris opened the truck door and jumped behind the steering wheel. Michael dove into the passenger seat.

"Hurry up," Michael bellowed. "Go!"

Chris couldn't close his shaking fingers over the keys. He tried to jam them into the ignition and dropped them.

"What's the matter?" Michael asked.

"I've never driven before."

"I drive Dad's truck all the time. Get out!"

"I'm so not surprised," Chris whimpered.

"Hurry!" Michael yelled.

Chris jumped out, careened around the truck, and front-ended Michael, knocking them to the floor and firing stars inside Chris' head. "What is this? Looney Tunes?"

Chris dove into the truck, slamming the door behind him. Michael jumped in and buckled his seat belt. "Go, stupid!" Chris shouted. "Uh, hold it. Where's the garage door opener?"

Bill burst threw the door and ran for the truck. Chris hit the locks just as he grabbed the door handle.

Michael threw the cherry Avalanche into reverse and stomped on the gas with both feet, dragging Bill with them. The truck hit the garage door with a deafening screech, like scissor blades scraped across a chalk board.

Chris crumpled onto the floorboard like a paper ball, smacking his head on the way down. He crawled up as the glove box popped open and cracked onto his head.

"Damn!" he screamed, slamming the box closed. He grabbed the seat top and peered out the back window.

The garage door stuck to the tailgate. Michael careened the truck into the street and stomped on the brakes. The door flew into a dump truck barreling at them.

"Go, Michael! Go!"

Michael slammed the truck into drive and screeched down the road as the dump truck veered into their garage. The garage roof folded, blowing a cloud of dust into the street.

"Like being five years old again," Michael said.

Chris swung into his seat.

"Hurry, Michael."

Michael crushed the accelerator. Chris grabbed his seat belt and yanked. The lock mechanism snapped it short, jarring his hands and burning his palms. Michael swung the steering wheel, throwing Chris' head into the side window as the back wheels skidded across the pavement and pulled them into a 360. The truck clipped a stop sign. It popped into the air, somersaulted, and slammed into the hood.

"You're gonna hurt someone!" Chris bellowed. "Slow down! Hold on. I've got a plan. Turn right at the end of this street."

Michael sped down the street and turned onto a two-lane highway.

"About fifteen miles," Chris said. "I'll tell you when."

A field of golden yellow canola, surrounded by a barbed wire fence, opened up on Chris' side. He turned around and looked behind them. The road was empty.

"Hurry, Michael. They'll see us on this straight stretch."

Michael stomped on the accelerator with a thump, pushing Chris into his seat.

Chris stared over the steering wheel into a packed coniferous forest on the north side of the highway. The darkened space under the canopy of pine needles blurred his vision. He felt sick. He pressed forward and raised his hand to fend off the sun.

"Only one chance," he whispered.

"Right here, Michael! Turn left. Quick!"

"Right?"

"LEFT!"

The tires shuddered over the hot asphalt like styrofoam pulled over glass. The Avalanche plowed into a wall of lilac bushes, blowing purple flowerets into a mushroom cloud and filling the cab with an odor of perfume and honey. Branches shrieked down the truck sides. Chris' head bashed the roof. The truck flew through the air.

The shock absorbers bottomed out and Chris felt the force of the landing up through his spine.

"Puh!" Michael's chest slammed into the steering wheel.

"Ouch! Stop the truck!" Chris ordered.

Michael stood on the brakes. Chris threw open the door, vanished into a sea of grass, and rolled.

"Quick, Michael. Cover the tracks."

Chris dashed to the bushes. They showed few signs of disturbance.

"Resilient little buggers."

Michael grabbed dirt from the roadside and sprinkled it over the skid marks. Chris scattered the tire tracks cut into the gravel shoulder and dusted the flowers off the ground. He tugged at the broken grass stems and grimaced as they flopped back down.

Chris kicked the grass in anger. "Wow. Inspector Clouseau could spot this."

A bee-like hum rose from the road. Chris grabbed Michael, shoved him into the foliage, and jumped after him.

"Your T-shirt, Michael. It's red! Get back!"

Chris lay on his side. Lilac stems pushed into his kidney, flooding him with waves of dull pain. He clenched his teeth, crawled forward until the leaves thinned, and peered through the gaps between them. A caterpillar as big as his index finger, lime green with two yellow stripes and a spike on its back, munched a leaf just above his head. Chris could hear it crunch as it bit, like a rabbit eating a carrot. He stared at it.

"There was a bronze Hummer and a blue Camry outside," Michael whispered.

"Hummer," Chris said.

"That Hummer is sick," Michael said.

"We'll be sick when they fill us full of lead."

The Hummer grew from the road. Its hood bobbed.

"They tapped the brakes," Chris whispered.

Chris remembered the rose bushes around their elementary school. He cowered behind them just like now, hiding from the school gang. He was pathetic, sometimes so stressed he'd step out and let them beat him. Then, he'd blame himself.

Kuma drove. Bill sat behind him, pointing a machine gun out the window. He swung the gun muzzle toward the bushes.

"Won't they see us?" Michael whispered.

"Probably not. Trust me. I've been here before. Hiding from jerks like you."

"Don't be an idiot, Chris."

"What? Can't handle the truth?"

The Hummer slowed. Sunrays glinted off Kuma's glasses and into Chris' eyes like lasers. The gun fixated on him, moving back as the Hummer crawled forward. Chris drew up his feet, coiled his legs, and pressed into the earth.

The Hummer passed right in front. Bill's dimple sank as his frown deepened.

"Get ready," Chris whispered.

The Hummer sped up and shot down the road.

"Whew." Chris stood. "Let's go."

They jumped into the truck. Chris plugged in his seatbelt and pointed to a gap in the forest above them.

"Through there. It leads to Jane and Greg's house."

Michael grinned. "Jane and Greg's house. Good idea. And it came from you."

Chris glared at him. "Your... I... I have good ideas. For good causes, you jerk. Jeez, anyway, we have to find a way up the hill. It's too steep."

Michael switched the truck into four wheel drive, stomped on the gas, and propelled them up the embankment. Chris clawed at the roof behind him as the front tires bounced on the tree roots twisting from the dirt, almost flipping them back. Michael gunned the accelerator. The truck shot over the top, hung for a life cringing second, and slammed onto the rear wheels. It stood near straight up. Chris gasped, sure he'd seen his last day, before the front plummeted to the ground and bounced like a beach ball.

"You really wanna die, don't you?" Chris asked.

"Stop bein' a pussy. At least I can drive."

"Yeah. You're driving me nuts."

A road, not much wider than the truck, overgrown with green grass and littered with boulders, cut through the trees, turned to the left, and disappeared into the forest.

Chris grabbed the dash. "Oh no."

Michael grinned. "Whee!"

CHAPTER 6

Chris' hands ached and his head hurt. He had clutched the hold handle for more than half an hour as Michael careened through the forest like a teenager on a joy ride.

They slid around a sharp corner and bounced toward a tree. Michael jacked the steering wheel to the left, rocketing around the tree and charging into Jane and Greg's back yard.

Chris groaned. "I feel like tossed salad."

Michael slammed on the brakes, throwing Chris forward. Sod and moist, chocolate dirt plopped onto the hood as the truck slid over the spongy grass.

"Michael!"

"Nice place for a flower bed, doncha think?" Michael said.

Chris glared at him. "Park in the garage."

"Sure. Wanna open it first?"

Chris grinned. "I'm surprised you'd ask. Stop out front."

Jane and Greg's house was tucked into a five acre lot, sandwiched between an evergreen forest on the south side and the Keetchum River on the north.

Michael drove over the expanse of grass, around to the front of the house, and onto the paved driveway.

Chris jumped out and sauntered to the Tudor style home. Constructed of reused bricks, white stucco, and rough beams stained coffee brown, it warmed and relaxed him. Jane and Greg had been family friends for as long as he could remember. He glided over the cobblestone sidewalk, punched 1-3-1-9-8 into the front door lock, stepped through, and punched 1-1-2-3-9-5 into the alarm system key pad. He walked to the garage and pressed the garage door opener.

The truck squealed as Michael drove it inside. Chris cringed at the dented hood and gouged sides. His dad loved that truck.

Chris walked to the foyer, stopped, and looked up. The home's grandeur still humbled him. Cleverly designed, it looked small from the outside. His gaze danced up the double grand staircase. Rails capped with dark cherry wood and polished to a shine and steps of grey marble laced with pink streaks rose to the wood paneled hallway above. The staircase seemed to float.

"Jane? Greg?" Chris called.

Michael turned and looked at him. "I thought they were on holidays."

"They are. I was just hoping. Come on."

They bounded up the stairs two at a time. Chris glanced at the Steinway grand piano. It almost looked lonely. He was tempted to belt out a symphony. *Beethoven's 5th* would fit well. He hummed the tune as they glanced into Jane and Greg's cavernous bedroom. The king sized bed was made, the hot tub covered, and the weights set in their racks.

"Place is empty," Michael said.

"Yes. Aren't you the smart one."

Chris walked on to their room before Michael could respond and opened the door. They stayed overnight often and Jane and Greg had set it aside for them. With two queen sized beds, dressers, and a book case, it still had enough room and ceiling height for a game of 21. Greg had helped Chris install the basketball hoop and paint a miniature court onto the polished hardwood floor. Chris tossed the computer onto his bed and grabbed the basketball, throwing it into the hoop.

Michael sneered. "Lucky shot."

"You always say that. Leave the gidgit bag here."

They ran downstairs to the kitchen.

Michael swept his hands over the granite countertops. Black with pink streaks, they matched the tile floor.

Chris inhaled. He smelled hamburgers and could see a plate of them on the counter, two patties, sesame buns, bacon, lettuce and tomato. His stomach growled. "Geez, I'm hungry. I'm seeing food."

"With ya."

Michael dashed to the entertainment room. Chris followed. A ten foot projection screen filled the south wall. Sub-woofers large enough to communicate with all the elephants of the Sahara hid in the corners behind the burgundy leather couch. Cherry wood panels lined the walls to Chris' waist. Green wallpaper, made to absorb sound, continued up to cherry wood crown moldings at the ceiling.

Michael stopped and stared unblinking at the screen. His skin turned a shade of grey.

"You all right?" Chis asked.

Michael rotated his head and looked with a vacant stare. "Uh, yeah."

"Okay. I'm going to the library. Call if you need me."

Chris left and walked down the hall to the library. He stood in the middle of the room and swirled in admiration. A bow window, crafted from dozens of book sized pieces of glass and soldered together with lead, towered above his head and splashed the room with sunlight. He squinted. Polished wood shelves packed with hard cover books met the ceiling. They sat quietly, as all books do, almost begging Chris to read them.

Chris paced over the hardwood floor. What would they do now? Michael almost got killed. Their parents were missing. Jane and Greg were gone. And Attila the Hun and his gang of idiots were chasing them.

"Gah!"

"Michael?" It sounded like he'd been flushed down the toilet. Chris dashed into the hallway.

"Michael?"

Chris ran to the kitchen. Michael leaned on the island. His eyes bulged and he shook like he was possessed. He slid to the floor and hurled, flooding the tile floor with a lake of digested nacho chips. Chris stopped, half expecting Michael's head to spin around.

"I can feel the bullets, Chris. They're in my legs, my back. God, they hurt!"

"You got hit?"

"NO! But I can feel them." Michael spewed again.

"I can't remember Mom's face, Chris. I can't remember what she looks like!" Tears streamed down his cheeks.

Chris walked into the puke. Leeching into his socks, it felt like warm dish soap. He leaned down and wrapped his arms around

Michael's shoulders. "Ssshhhh. It'll be all right. We'll get help."

"From who? Who do we go to?"

"The police?"

Michael rocked on his knees. "You know what'll happen, Chris. They'll toss us into foster care."

"Yeah, I know. Let's hide out for a while. Maybe we can figure out what's going on. Here, help me clean up this mess. I'm going to cut the grass."

"You're what?"

Chris jumped up and wiped his hands on his jeans. "Cut the grass. I promised Jane and Greg I would, and this might be my only chance."

Chris walked across the back yard toward the shed. They had cleaned up the puke, which took care of Chris' appetite, and Michael had calmed down. Chris left him in the entertainment room to unwind.

Chris smiled as he stepped to the shed. Although sided with rough-hewn lumber and looking abandoned, it was the size of a small house. He unlocked the door and entered a woodwork shop. He stopped and breathed deep, absorbing the sawdust and varnish.

The walls were lined with cabinets, many crafted by himself, and he grinned with pride. Greg taught him with kindness and patience. He picked out the cabinets made by Michael, who was fascinated by the tools, but not so much the time needed to perfect his creations.

Chris was happy when Jane asked him to watch their house. She and Greg left last week to visit her brother. He lived on an island somewhere on the West Coast. Greg taught Chris how to use the lawn mower and Jane showed him how to water the plants and arm the security system. He grinned, having looked forward to driving the lawn mower. After Michael's driving it didn't seem exciting anymore.

Jane had always been kind to them. Her blonde hair flowed and blue eyes danced like a mountain stream. Often, she shed tears as he and Michael left for home, which was strange. She looked bitter when she cried.

Chris was surprised Michael couldn't remember their mom. Was he in shock? She shared Michael's emerald eyes. She was slender and tall with auburn hair, and her skin would never need a tanning bed. A striking combination. Their mother exuded intelligence, and Chris imagined her job at the research centre involved complex and twisted science stuff. But as a mother, she sucked.

Chris weaved through the band saw, planer, and table saw to the back, where the lawn mower seemed to wait in anticipation. He unlatched and opened a metal garage door. It screeched over galvanized rails and folded above his head, allowing the sunlight to burst through. Chris squinted, sat on the lawn mower, and turned the key. It purred and scuttled outside, pressing him into the seat. He pulled his foot off the throttle, surprised by the acceleration. He swung the steering wheel left, then right, like a cat chasing a toy mouse. He pulled a donut around the Mountain Ash tree, and regaining his confidence, set to cutting the grass.

He cut three swaths, and with each blade of grass scythed by the spinning blades, his nerves heightened. He felt someone watching him. He peered into the forest. The trees seemed to march inwards, encircling, leaning over, and threatening. He bit his lip to stop the quiver in his chin. A space, vast and lonely, expanded from his stomach and into his throat, creating a lump he couldn't swallow. He squeezed his eyes and forced back tears.

Who can I turn to? What if Michael gets hurt or killed?

Blood red clippings spewed from under the mower. "Doh! Petunias. Shoot. The flower bed. Get a grip, Chris!" He stopped the mower, wiped his eyes with his shirt, and stared into the sky.

What if they come here? How will we even know? I'll get Michael to rig an alarm system. And we'll need an escape route.

He steered the mower to the north side of the acreage and peered down a hill sparsely covered with silver birch trees growing among a carpet of crunchy grass. A path, cut into the escarpment, led from the garage side door to a dock suspended alongside the riverbank. Jane and Greg's jet boat was docked down there. Greg let Chris drive it last summer.

Yes! Chris thought. Have to set it up, then figure out what's going on. First, the grass. He stepped on the throttle and started a new swath. His thoughts faded into the sun's warmth and aroma of freshly cut grass.

The lawn cut, Chris opened the back door and strutted into the entertainment room. Michael bounced on the couch. With a series of lethal karate kicks, he was beating an Org to a defenseless pulp.

"Is this all you've done for the past hour?" Chris asked.

"Pretty much."

"Shut it down. I've got a plan."

Michael's brow furrowed. His avatar guy got kicked in the head. "What?"

"We should install an alarm at the front gate and prepare a getaway."

"'Larms taken care of," Michael muttered while pulling the controller into his stomach and raising his right knee above his head.

"Whadya mean?"

"Wanna see it? It's brilliant. Like me." Michael paused the game and set the controller beside him.

"Sure," Chris whispered.

Michael jumped up and led Chris out the front door. They wandered down the paved lane snaking from the house. Chris peered into the forest. He didn't like the shadows. They moved. Something was out there. He felt like a cat creeping through a dog pound.

The gate was eighteen feet ahead. Twenty-four black iron rods tipped with a gold arrow were welded together to form a nine-foot tall barrier. Brick pillars book-ended the gate, each supporting a marble lion. A grey electrical enclosure and a motor, installed by the right pillar, opened and closed it. Michael led Chris into the forest, around the gate, and to the outside.

"I re-routed the gate intercom wires into the house alarm. It'll trigger if someone approaches. As well, I added a module that sends a frequency signal. The signal is picked up by this walkie-talkie. We need to carry it with us."

"Oh. Aren't you smart," Chris muttered.

"You'll get used to it, Chris. I used the garage door infra red sensors. Michael pointed across the road at the base of two trees. I installed the beams over there and the sensors here beside the gate.

"The sensors pick up the infra-red light. If it's blocked by a vehicle, it'll send an alarm."

Chris waved his arm in front of a sensor. "Like this?"

"Close. To make sure a deer doesn't trigger the alarm, I set it up so both have to be blocked. Here, you stand in front of that one and I'll stand in front of this one."

The walkie-talkie blared: "I love you. You..."

"Barney? Quick!" Chris yelled. "Turn it off! Turn it off!"

"Designed to wake the dead." Michael grabbed the walkie-talkie and turned the volume down.

"Good job, Michael. A vehicle or a lowly pair of deer will drive us to near insanity."

"Good point," Michael said. "I hope deer don't travel in pairs."

"I'll never get that song out of my head!" Chris muttered. "Let's booby trap the place and get the boat ready."

Chris squatted on the dock and surveyed the Sea-Doo Utopia jet boat. His stomach swirled. He had chewed off his index fingernail to the skin. He was preparing to steal Jane and Greg's boat, and it felt bad.

The sun tipped behind the treetops; it had taken two hours to set the booby traps. Michael was in the house looking for camping equipment.

The boat crouched like a tiger ready to spring, its tip elevated and its stern curling down and almost folding under the river's surface. A cherry stripe slid down its nineteen foot length, painted over a shiny, butterscotch fuselage. A split, cantilevered bench made room for three at the dash. Three could sit in the back and two in the stern. Twin two hundred and fifteen horsepower motors drove the jet propulsion system. Chris didn't know how fast it could go. Greg once coaxed him to fifty miles an hour.

He rubbed his arms, recalling the first time he pulled the throttle. The boat snapped forward with such vigor his elbows cracked. His arms were stiff after that.

He hopped in and checked the fuel gauge. It indicated full. He started the engine. It growled. "Great!" He turned it off and left the key in the ignition. He hiked up the path, side-stepping the booby traps and entered the house through the garage door. Running through the kitchen to the laundry room at back, he plunged down a set of stairs into an unfinished basement to find Michael surrounded by camping equipment.

"Keep digging, Michael. I'll create a list."

Chris grabbed the red backpack. "This one's yours." He placed it on the floor, grabbed a blue backpack, and tossed it beside the red one. He pulled a sleeping bag from the pile and threw it by Michael's pack. He wrote it down on a pad of paper.

Thirty minutes had passed. Chris glanced through the list, looking for missed items.

Backpack x 2
Sleeping bag and mat x 2
Tent
Hatchet
Matches
Newspaper
Rain jackets
Toothpaste, toothbrushes
Pots and pans
Plates and cups
Tea Towel
Dish soap, pot scrubber
Stove and fuel
Water filter
Water bottles
Knives
First Aid Kit
Mirror
Map
Compass
Socks
T-Shirts
Can opener
"Okay, Michael. Stuff it in."

They filled the packs and pulled them up the stairs. "Whew, this thing's heavy," Michael said as he dragged his pack over the kitchen floor.

"Wait till we add the food. Into the pantry and toss some out. I'll tell you when to stop."

Chris placed the pad and pen on the island. Michael disappeared into the pantry door.

A box of Kraft Dinner flew out and smacked Chris' head.

"Ouch! I didn't mean it literarily. Jeez, Michael, just put the stuff on the island."

Michael popped his head out of the pantry. "You can throw a basketball, but can't catch a simple box of KD?"

"Just give me the damn food."

As Michael passed the food out, Chris wrote it on a list and placed it into a waterproof nylon bag.

Kraft dinner
Oatmeal
Pop-tarts
Powered milk
Chocolate bars
Potato chips
Trail mix
Canned ham and tuna
Ketchup
Pop

"Chris!" Michael cried, holding up a bottle of rum. "Cuba Libra?"

"No!"

Michael unscrewed the cap. "If I'm gonna die, I wanna try a drink of rum before I go." He pressed the bottle to his lips, took a long gulp, and gagged.

"Gah! This stuff tastes like Buckleys!"

"Gimme that," Chris said. He grabbed the bottle and took a sip. Fire slid down his throat and dropped into his stomach like a donut into a fryer.

Chris grimaced. "Yak! Not Buckleys, furniture polish."

Michael looked at him and raised his eyebrows. "You've drunk furniture polish?"

"That story stays with me, come on. Let's put this stuff in the boat."

Chris grabbed two steaks from the freezer, placed them into the microwave, and watched the defrost time out. It was seven o'clock, and he was tired and hungry, but pleased they had finished their chores.

Michael walked into the kitchen. "I'm going to find some cash."

Chris jumped as the microwave beeped. "Make sure you put an I.O.U. in its place."

Michael thumped up the stairs. Chris pulled out the steaks. They were bloody and wet, marbled with fat, and pulled images of Michael's bullet riddled body into his head. His hand started to shake and he dropped the plate on the island with a clatter. Michael should have died today. How did he escape those bullets anyway? Bill shot from twenty feet away, and he obliterated the wall. Michael had always been lucky and, for once, Chris was glad for it, though Michael's fear shocked him. He'd never seen Michael scared of anything, until today.

Chris fired up the grill and tossed on the steaks. The flames devoured the dripping fat, and the smells kicked Chris' appetite into overdrive, pushing the horrific pictures from his mind. He placed two potatoes into the oven and a pot of water on the stove for beans. He'd been cooking dinner for years, leaving Michael's on a plate for whenever he'd get home. Michael had never thanked him. Instead he chased Chris out of the kitchen with his ghostly noises, clanging pans, and blinking lights. Chris shook his head, his anger dissipating over the thought that Michael was so darned clever. He removed the steaks and placed each on a plate.

"Chris!"

"What?" Chris turned off the burners and bounded up to Jane and Greg's room. Michael sat on their bed, staring at two large binders, one decorated with ivory lace, the other with blue.

"Look, Chris, from when we were born."

Chris grabbed the blue binder and opened it. The first page displayed a baby's footprint with his name and birth date written below it. The next page displayed a picture of him, just after he was born, he assumed. His tiny head was squashed and red all over. He flipped forward to his grade two school picture. Even then, his brown eyes peeked through a curtain of long, black hair, looking haunted and unhappy. He was short and chubby in grade two, a far cry from his lean six foot frame now. He was proud to be the tallest fourteen year old kid at school. The bullies left him alone after he outgrew them.

"Holy, Michael. They have three pages of pictures for every year of my life."

"Yeah, me, too," Michael whispered.

"Look, Chris. Here's one of you holding me when I was a baby. You sure were beaming."

"Yeah. I was really proud, Michael. I was going to teach you everything you... did, did you find cash?"

"Yep. Two hundred."

"Good. Food's ready. Let's eat."

Chris watched Michael pile his plate with green beans. He opened the oven and tossed Michael a potato. He scooped some beans onto his plate, split open a potato, and gobbed peanut butter on it. They walked to the TV room and flopped onto the couch.

Michael grabbed the remote and turned on the TV. "What the...?"

CHAPTER 7

The sound of helicopter blades blew out of the speakers and Chris ducked, half expecting a helicopter to crash into the room.

Their house spun on the TV screen, projected from a helicopter circling above. The garage roof rested on top of the dump truck. Shingles, rain gutters, splintered wood, and glass carpeted their grass and driveway, and the neighbor's front porch. Police cars packed the street. Red and blue lights swirled off windows like glitter dust. A dozen officers enclosed in yellow ribbon milled around the yard. A large crowd had gathered on the sidewalk and boulevard.

A staccato voice barked a reporter's rendition of the events.

"Police are coordinating a manhunt for the two missing boys, Michael, twelve, and Chris, fourteen. Officers are posted at all bus and train stations. Please contact the police if you see these young men," the reporter said.

Chris and Michael's faces filled the screen; oily skin, zits, freckles, and unwashed hair. They looked like two circus clowns posing for a mug shot. Chris prickled with embarrassment.

"You look criminal," Michael said.

"At least I didn't just get my hair cut," Chris stuttered. "You look like a bald pansy."

"Pansy? Are you kid..."

"Shush, listen."

"Let's return to Jaydon with her report from the street," the anchorman said.

"Must be her first report," Chris muttered.

37

Jaydon's eyes flooded their room with panic. Red blotches surfaced and spread over her cheeks and neck. She seemed to be looking at the wrong camera.

"Thanks, John. Police are searching for their uh," she glanced down at her notebook, "parents, Claire and Geoff Boulton." She glanced again and paused.

"Uh, Claire and Geoff were both at work on Friday. Fellow workers informed me they have acted perfectly normally although Claire was quite distraught after her older son Chris was apparently attacked by a gopher? We understand he received substantial injuries to his testicles as a result of this attack."

Chris sucked in and a chunk of steak lodged in his throat. He coughed and blew it across the room onto the screen.

"They can't say that? On TV? What? Can they?" He squealed.

"Am I gonna to have to perform the Heimlich?" Michael asked.

"Shut up!" Chris yelled. "My testicles are on national television because of you!"

"Least they're not displaying a mug shot of those." Michael rolled off the couch and squealed with laughter.

Chris grew hot and sticky. His hands and legs started to shake. He stomped to the screen and wiped the steak blood off with his napkin.

Jaydon continued. "Sources told me the house is ransacked. Furniture is broken, walls are riddled with bullets, floors are covered with blood. Even ceiling tiles have been pulled down."

"Have the police given any clue as to what this is about, Jaydon?" the anchorman asked.

"Not really, John. Other than a bulletin about the missing boys, the police are tight-lipped. I asked several officers on the street for information, but they divulged nothing. Let's talk to some local residents. Maybe we can dig something up.

"You!" she yelled to a boy standing across from her. "What do you think of all this excitement in your neighborhood?"

Chris gasped as the camera zoomed in on the boy.

"I think Michael's a jerk! He deserves whatever he has coming to him!"

"Oh! Ah, John, back to you. I think I found a suspect."

"Ha! I told you he'd pay you back," Chris exclaimed, and grinned.

Michael, a red hue engulfing his face, grabbed a pillow and whipped it at Chris' head.

"Thomas. I'll kill him when I get back."

"Kinda proves his point, doesn't it?"

Michael glared. "Do you wanna live?"

The station cut to John, the anchorman. White hair, dim eyes, hairy ears, and a large, mottled nose were accentuated with Coke bottle glasses, a green suit and tie, and an orange shirt unbuttoned around his neck. He sucked air into his lungs, an obvious attempt to expand his presence. A button popped off his suit jacket and pinged into the camera lens.

"In other news, Robert Cain, the wealthy billionaire, flew direct from his private West Coast island to Silvertip this morning. Gord, our business reporter, tracked down Robert Cain at the luxurious Notlih Hotel where Robert rented the entire top floor for the week. Gord, over to you."

Gord wheezed through the hotel parking lot. The sun glared off his polished head. His staggering bulk filled the TV. The camera weaved and bobbed behind him, trying to zero in on Robert Cain.

"Heh. A bowling pin with undersized legs," Michael said.

"Shush."

Robert, surrounded by a half dozen men dressed in black suits, white shirts with black ties, and black polished shoes, walked a fast march. They twisted their heads in all directions, peering through dark sunglasses, looking for signs of an attack, Chris guessed. Each guard's right hand was tucked inside his jacket. Robert, visible in the center of the mob, was identically dressed.

"Mr. Cain?" Gord squealed. "Do you have any comments? What brings you to our fine town? Are you making any donations? We need a new recreational center!"

Robert Cain surged on. Panting louder, Gord accelerated the chase.

A bronze Hummer popped into view and crawled toward them. Robert and his pack stopped like an army of robots. Robert turned, broke through his men, and approached the reporter.

"That's the Hum" Michael exclaimed as the camera panned to Robert. "Did you see it?"

"Yeah, for a second. It sure looked the same. How many bronze Hummers can there be in a small town like Silvertip?"

About six feet tall, with a medium build and military shoulders, Robert Cain sprinted toward the camera. His small featured face, blue eyes, and neatly cut black hair came into focus as he squared into view. If he was breathing, Chris couldn't see. His striking looks were tainted by an air of malice. Chris shivered and squirmed, squeaking against the leather couch.

"I've come to Silvertip for business meetings. Yes, I'd love to build a recreational centre for your fine city. My secretary will contact your mayor and get it started."

Robert glanced to his left, clenched his teeth, swiveled, and dashed away.

"That wraps my report, John. About naming that new centre, I think the Gord Witchim Sports Centre sounds just fine, don't you?"

"Yeah, sure, thanks, Gord. Let's take a commercial break. Janice will return with the weather report."

"I have to check this guy out," Chris said. "There's something fishy about him." Chris turned off the TV. "Come on, Michael, I'll wash, you dry."

Michael rolled his eyes. "You're such a suck. Who says we have to do dishes?"

"It's about time you started helping. I'm tired of doing everything for you."

Chris dumped the dishes into the sink, squirted in some soap, and started the water. He grabbed a towel and threw it at Michael's head. "So, what's the plan for tomorrow?"

Michael pulled the towel off his face and glared. "I'm gonna kill you before they do. Go scan Jane and Greg's computer, and my copy of Mom and Dad's."

"What are we looking for?"

Michael grabbed a clean plate from Chris and started drying it. "No doubt, Mom and Dad are involved with some nasty people. Whatever they're up to, I'm sure there's evidence of it somewhere."

"And Jane and Greg?"

"Same, assuming they're involved somehow."

Chris placed the forks and knives in the drying rack and pulled the plug. "I can't believe any of this. Mom and Dad work a lot, but they can't be into something illegal, can they?"

"Dunno what to think. I hope we find out before Kuma finds us, though."

Chris put the plates in the cupboard and they skulked up to their bedroom. Michael turned out the lights, flooding the room in darkness, and ran across the room and jumped into bed.

Chris stared at the ceiling. Howling winds whacked pine branches into their window. Every swish and creak pushed Kuma into his thoughts. Chris wondered where Kuma was now. Could he be at the gate this very instant?

Chris rubbed his eyes, peered through pinched eyelashes, and allowed the sunlight to break through. Toasty under the comforter, he pulled it to his chin and squirmed into the mattress. He felt like a five-year-old. Small things, normally unnoticed, devoured him; the walls, painted sky blue, cast a pinkish tinge; the polished oak book shelf sparkled with sunlight; a crack marred the white stucco ceiling.

A chestnut squirrel hopped on a pine branch outside their window, a thin branch, laden with heavy bunches of pine needles, clumped together like miniature porcupines, and decorated with the odd pinecone. The squirrel stretched over its little hands and touched its nose to the window. The branch bobbed, giving the squirrel a comical appearance, like he bounced on a diving board. It twitched its tail, opened its mouth, and baring its pink tongue scolded Chris like a machine gun.

Chris grinned. The squirrel puffed its chest, raised its rear, and formed a question mark with its tail when it scolded.

"Shush," Chris whispered.

He peered at the clock on the wall.

"Holy cow! Ten o'clock."

He scanned the room. Michael was gone.

Chris pushed his leg into the warm bedroom air and allowed gravity to pull him to the floor. He tugged on his jeans and T-shirt and ran downstairs to the kitchen. Michael held up a plate stacked with pancakes and smiled.

"Wow, those are massive. I didn't know you could cook. What's in them?"

"M&Ms, marshmallows, and cashews. I found strawberry jam, whipped cream, and chocolate syrup to spread on top."

Chris patted his stomach. "Hmmm. Breakfast of the gods."

Chris demolished three pancakes, Michael four. They jumped up and cleaned the kitchen, eager to start their task.

"I'll take Mom and Dad's computer, you take Jane and Greg's," Michael commanded. "Check documents, e-mails, pictures, and videos. Look for anything suspicious." Michael rubbed his tummy and grimaced. "Geez, I think I'm gonna blow up."

Chris leaned back over his chair and stretched. He checked his watch. "Four hours! Holy!" His stomach growled. He padded to the kitchen and opened the pantry door. Foraging for munchies, he found a monster bag of nachos on the floor behind the sack of potatoes and on top of a bag of flour. Grabbing a Coke from the fridge, he clambered onto an island barstool and tore the nachos open.

His hands were shaking, and he realized how exhausted he was. Last night he lay trembling, listening in fear for the Barney song until the sun rose. Waiting for Barney was as close to torture as he ever wanted to get; leave it to Michael to come up with an idea like that. At least, with a lifetime of Michael's antics, he was used to fear, but not this kind of fear. Regardless of how Michael had treated him, Chris had a close attachment to him, and being responsible for Michael's life sucked.

He glanced into the bag, half empty.

"Ah-well," he muttered. Grabbing the bag of chips, he headed back to the computer. He had found a strange e-mail between his dad and Greg. Sitting down, he pulled it up and started reading it from the bottom up.

Greg. We're really close. I sent the fruit fly ahead, one minute. It disappeared, then appeared again. Used a ton of power, though. I'm not sure how we'll test it on a mammal.
Geoff

Hey, Geoff. Sounds promising. Only took ya ten years. (: Do you need more power then? We can't rely on the grid much longer. Gas fired turbine?
Greg

That'll be big bucks, Greg.
Geoff

I'll see what I can do. Fix up a demo.
Greg.

Greg and their dad were good friends, but Chris had no idea Greg was involved in the lab.

"I got it! Chris! I've got it!"

Chris jumped from his chair and dashed out of their room, nachos clutched in his hand, and ran to Michael. "You've got what?"

"Look at this!"

Michael's eyes danced with excitement, and his face was flushed. Chris scanned the text filling the monitor.

"Jane Cain. So what, who's she?" Chris asked, feeling deflated.

Michael's eyes sparkled. "Hold on. I'll show you her photograph. I found it on the Internet." He popped open a second Explorer window.

A wave of dizziness struck Chris. He grabbed the back of Michael's chair. "Is this some kind of joke?"

"Nope, checks out."

"Jane? Our Jane? Jane's brother is a billionaire? No, can't be. Are you sure?

"Yep. Robert Cain is Jane's brother."

Chris pulled up a chair and sat down. "That just doesn't make sense," he whispered.

Michael pulled back from the screen. "I don't get it. Jane and Greg left to visit her brother. If Robert is her brother and Jane went to see him, what's he doing here?"

"Another brother?"

"I checked. There were only two kids," Michael said.

"And Robert Cain?"

"He's not a self made billionaire. He inherited his fortune from his dad. At least that's what it says on the news reports."

"Their mother?"

"She died when Jane was eight years old. But, if Robert inherited billions Jane would have too. She wouldn't buy me an IPod for Christmas. If she was a billionaire she'd have got me a Beamer to go with it."

"Dunno, weird, I wonder if Robert ducked that Hummer on purpose."

"You don't think they're related?" Michael asked.

"Robert and the Hummer?"

"Who else?"

"Could be," Chris trailed off in thought. "Where did Kuma say they were taking Mom and Dad?"

"Um, I think he said, back to the island."

"Yes! He said about an hour's flight. How far is Robert's island from here?"

Michael called up Google maps and zoomed onto the West Coast. "Here, the city of Coruntan is on the coast, about four hundred and fifty miles."

A pang of excitement streaked through Chris' stomach. "A jet could do four hundred and fifty miles in an hour."

"You don't think they're on that island, do you? I mean, what could Jane and Greg possibly have to do with Mom and Dad's disappearance?"

They stared at the screen.

Chris walked behind the computer and faced Michael. "You know what we have to do?"

"Uh, no."

"Get to that island."

Michael's face turned red. "Are you nuts? Coruntan? Four hundred and fifty miles?"

"Why so angry, Michael. What else can we do?"

"I... I... but four hundred and fifty miles? No way, Chris!"

"You want to wait here then?"

"No, but..."

"There's maps in the kitchen drawer. See what you can find on Google. I know they're there!" Chris dashed to the kitchen. He was surprised by Michael's concern. Michael would jump into a pool of sharks if dared to do it, where as Chris planned his trips to the bathroom. He pulled open a drawer by the refrigerator and dug through the maps. "Aha! Got one." He grabbed some highlighters from the pencil cup, ran upstairs, and spread the map out on the table. Placing the highlighter at Silvertip, he ran it over the river to the town of Skyler. "Michael. Call this up on Google. How far?"

"We're going over the mountains?" Michael asked.

"We don't have much choice, do we? The island's on the other side."

Chris placed the laptop, maps, and markers into the computer bag. He yawned and rubbed his eyes; they were dry and sore. He checked his watch. It was midnight. "We've been at this for six hours.

Let's go." He turned off the computer and stumbled toward the door, leading Michael upstairs. Peeling off his jeans and T-shirt, he crawled into bed, turned onto his back, and stared into black.

"Chris?"

"Uh-huh?"

"Are we nuts?"

"Let's get some sleep, Michael."

"What now?" Kuma asked over the cell phone while swinging the Hummer onto a residential street. Kuma clenched his fist and rubbed his eyes. It was late. They had searched for the boys all day.

"Ditch the Hummer, you idiot. What were you thinking?"

Kuma sat up in his seat. "Uh, yeah. I didn't expect to find a reporter there."

"Another stupid move like that and fish'll be eating your eyes. Ditch the wheels."

"I like the Hummer. Can I get a red one?"

"Sure. Did you check Jane and Greg's house?"

"No. Where is it?"

"Idiot. I told you to go there first. Big acreage alongside the river. Beautiful house. I'll give you the address. It'll be on your GPS."

CHAPTER 8

Chris lay in bed and listened. Was he dreaming? He could hear his parents. They were downstairs in the kitchen. The smell of coffee and bacon wafted through the hall and into his bedroom. His tummy rumbled and pulsated under his hand. His dad must be cooking. He always did on those rare mornings they stayed home.

His dad was a tall, lanky man. A black goatee that bobbed when he chewed, shiny brown eyes, and an overactive smile created a well of confidence that one felt more than saw. Quiet and unassuming, as though deep in thought, he rarely talked, but when he did those around paid close attention. He made people laugh, often at themselves.

Chris rolled onto his back and gazed into the crack. It extended over the ceiling like a tree branch.

Birds twittered outside. It's gonna be hot and sunny today.

Michael was watching TV, he surmised. He listened to the catchy tune.

I love youuu. You love meee.

Chris hated that song. Is he trying to torture me or does he really like that show?

We're a happy...

"Guh, why me?"

He rolled over and drifted back to sleep.

"Uh!"

Something poked his ribs, hard.

"Chris, wake up."

He popped open his eyes and stared into Michael's nostrils. Funny, he'd never noticed hair in Michael's nostrils before.

"What?"

Michael's hair was drenched with sweat, his hands shaking, and his eyes wide and unblinking.

"We slept through it, Chris, Barney. They're outside the house. I heard their car doors."

"Outside?"

Chris' stomach flipped. He bounded out of bed, threw his feet into his jeans, grabbed the waistband, and stepped forward while pulling them on. His left foot stuck. Like a tree clinging to gravity after the fatal chop of an axe, he paused, full in despair of what was about to occur, before falling over and crashing onto his head with a thud.

"Shush! They'll hear you. I'll grab the laptop," Michael said.

The pain washed away with adrenalin, Chris pulled on his T-shirt, socks, and shoes; he checked his watch.

"Eleven o'clock, Michael. How did we sleep so long?"

He grabbed the gidgit bag and dashed down the hall, stopping at the top of the stairs and peering around the corner. Bill's face pressed into the frosted glass panel beside the front door.

Numbness spread through Chris' arms and legs. "It's Bill."

Feeling Michael's sweaty hair under his arm, Chris swung the gidgit bag into his face.

"Ouch! Come on, Chris. At least I know how to dress myself."

"Shush! Wait for my command."

"When did you become the boss? You're an idiot."

Bill disappeared.

Soft beeping noises crept up the stairs.

Chris glanced back at Michael. His heart pounded, his legs felt like diarrhea, and he didn't know what to do. "The door lock!"

Michael clenched his teeth. "Well, run! Now!"

Chris dove around the corner and leapt down the stairs.

"So much for a carefully planned getaway," Michael muttered.

The door flew open. Kuma's black eyes pierced Chris' like a scope on a gun.

Chris careened to the right and dashed toward the garage. He opened the door, turned, and looked into Michael's face. It was red. The blood vessels on his forehead bulged like a tuba. His eyes were so big they stretched his face, and he wasn't breathing, which caused his lips to cave in like he'd bitten a lemon and his cheeks to puff out.

Kuma reached toward Michael's neck.

Chris dashed through the doorway, waited for Michael to pass, and threw his weight onto the door, crashing it onto Kuma's arm.

"You little...!" Kuma yelled.

Chris cracked the door into Kuma's arm again. Kuma screamed and pulled it back.

"Let's go, let's go, let's go!" Chris punched the lock, pushed past Michael, streaked across the garage, and dove through the side door and onto the path.

They mumbled the practiced steps and hurled down -- "Step 1, step 2, step 3, right, step 1, step 2, left, duck, step 1,..."

Kuma slid to a stop and let his men thunder by. This would be over in seconds. The boys were right in front of them.

"Don't touch the tall one," he yelled. "He gets a personal beating from me!"

Joe hit the shin-height piano wire strung across the path and slammed onto his right knee and shoulder. His fingers, pinched between the gravel and his machine gun, shed a streak of skin and blood onto the path.

Pete jumped over Joe, looked back, and sliced into the chest-height piano wire. He swung up and hung. His arms fanned as he plummeted onto his back in a cloud of dust.

Ing jumped over Joe, under the piano wire, and over Pete. He leapt into a switchback, sliding off a piece of buried sheet metal. His right leg cracked into a birch tree, snapping his tibia with a sickening crunch. He threw himself back, squirmed, and screamed like a baby.

Kuma watched the boys and pulled out his cell phone.

"Just a couple of snot-nosed kids, eh?" he yelled while punching a phone number into the keypad.

CHAPTER 9

Chris pounced into the driver's seat and cranked the key.

Michael grappled with the rope. "Why did we tie this thing?" he yelled.

Machine gun bullets spewed into the water and thunked into the dock, blowing it into clouds of splinters.

"Hurry, Michael!"

"Go!" Michael screamed.

Chris gunned the boat. He heard a thump and glanced back. Michael was sprawled over the packs, his arms and legs flailing as he tried to find his balance.

"Whuh-hooo! That was fun!" Michael yelled.

Chris shook his head. Only Michael could call this fun. He spun the boat east. The bow shot into the air. The steering wheel slipped from his hand and he fell back, lodging his feet under the dash. He lunged forward and grabbed the wheel, fearful the boat would capsize. The bow dropped to the water and a forty foot plume blasted out behind them. Chris' neck snapped back and they shot forward.

"Are you trying to kill me?" Michael yelled.

Chris' heart hammered. He squeezed the throttle hard, trying to control his shaking hand, but lost control of the boat's speed instead, pitching it fast, then slow. He let go of the throttle and nudged it back with his fist, bringing the boat down to fifty miles an hour. He turned to the shores on the north side of the river, scanning them for the passage.

Michael grabbed the dash and crawled into his seat. "Where the heck are you going? We're supposed to be going west. That way!" he yelled while pointing behind them.

"Hold onto your shorts. You'll see."

Chris slowed the boat, yanked the steering wheel left, and plunged into a channel, heading west. "It runs along the river for four miles. Greg showed it to me last summer. It should throw off Kuma for a few hours."

The channel, just wider than the boat and shaded with willow trees, cast dark shadows over the still green water. It smelled like compost.

Chris ducked as a branch slapped the windshield and tossed the boat through a sharp turn. Michael gripped the dash with wide-eyed terror. Chris grinned, gunned the boat, and cranked the steering wheel out of control, sliding into a turn just before hitting a tree. Michael sunk farther into his seat. Scaring the crap out of Michael felt like floating, drinking a chocolate shake, and watching Saturday morning cartoons at the same time. Chris laughed above the engine's roar.

Michael stared at him. "You okay?"

Chris grinned. "What? I trusted your driving yesterday."

A fallen tree, reaching across the river's surface, popped into view. He slammed the throttle back, dropping the bow into the water and stopping the boat on the spot, throwing Michael into the windshield. Michael stood and glared as the tree thwacked into his chest and tossed him into the river.

"Jeez, I'm in trouble now." Chris swung the boat to where Michael had disappeared. Ducking under the tree, he cut the engine. A plume of grey muck ballooned and spread over the water's surface.

"Where are you?" He started to worry. It felt like a minute had passed.

Michael sloshed to the surface, coughing and gagging. Pulling grey slime off his head, he dragged it through his eyes. "Damn you, Chris!"

Chris pulled a life preserver from under the back seat and tossed it. "Grab it, Michael!"

Chris pulled Michael toward the boat, gripped his pants, and hauled him onto the floor with a thud.

"Am I gonna have to give you mouth to mouth? Are you all

right?"

Michael spat water onto Chris' feet. "I'm fine. And don't you touch me!"

"I stopped the boat for a reason, twit. If you'd looked ahead instead of glaring at me, that wouldn't have happened. Anyway, let's get going." Chris jumped into his seat. "It'll take two hours to get to Skylar."

Chris blew out of the tributary and accelerated to sixty. He glanced at the whirlpools dotting the river's calm surface and cringed. His friend Tanner had tried to swim across the river on a dare. He was half a mile downstream when an undercurrent sucked him under. They found his body two days later, under the surface snagged on a fallen tree. Chris had tried to talk him out of the stunt. He would never forget the grin on Tanner's face as he slipped into the water and started to swim. Tanner was the opposite of Chris. He was happy about everything, it seemed. And then he was gone. Chris swallowed the lump in his throat and rubbed tears from his eyes.

The wind warmed Chris' face. The motor's noise cracked over the water and echoed off the shoreline. They hadn't talked since leaving the tributary two hours ago. Michael scanned the north road for suspicious vehicles and the sky for helicopters.

They roared up to Skylar, a town of five thousand nestled beneath low lying mountains. Treeless, the area was covered with yellow grass and blue sage brush. The south shore opposite the town opened to a dairy farm. Black and white Jersey cows looked up all at the same time as they roared by, along with the Skylar residents swimming along the shore. Chris grinned. There was something funny about the scene, like a Far Side cartoon.

"Look at the Jersey cows, Michael."

Michael looked at Chris and grinned. "Holsteins."

"Hole what?" Chris asked.

"Holsteins are black. Jersey cows are brown."

Chris shook his head. Outdone again, he felt angry. "Cows? Really, Michael?"

"Don't be a hater Chris. Look." Michael raised his arm and pointed at the beach. "There must be eighty kids in there."

Chris scanned the beach. Kuma could be watching them at that very moment, and they were announcing their arrival in a flashy jet boat. He throttled back.

"How long has it been?" Michael asked.

"It's two o'clock."

"I'm hungry," Michael said.

"Me too, and we should get some gas."

Chris pulled the boat toward the town dock.

It was five o'clock and the sun bore into Chris' eyes. He grabbed his sunglasses from a cup holder and slid them on. His ears rang from the engine noise, and his body vibrated with the boat. He was tired, and his hands and arms were sore. They had filled up with gas at Skylar, bought subs, and walked the stiffness out of their legs while eating. It seemed like an eternity had passed since they left Skylar. He was bored, which was strange. How could he be bored when chased by a gang of killers? This was when they'd get killed, numbed by sunshine, wind, and noise, and not paying attention.

"Ouch!" Michael screamed. Chris popped from his daydream to find Michael pulling a large, black beetle off his forehead. The sticky entrails stuck to his skin like a string of chewed gum.

Chris laughed. "You make a great windshield. There's a red dot between your eyes."

"There'll be red blood splattered all over your face if you wanna try and laugh again."

Chris clenched his teeth. Michael could never take a joke if it was at his expense.

"Chris!" Michael stared into the sky.

"What?"

"Up there." Michael pointed high and ahead. A black dot materialized from the grainy sky. Was it a bird? It grew awfully fast.

Michael ducked behind the dash. "Cover!"

Chris swung the boat to his left and gunned for the riverbank, sliding the boat under a patch of willows leaning over the river. He throttled down.

A branch slapped Michael across the face. He grimaced, grabbed it, and pulled. The boat swung in and rested against the muddy shoreline.

They breathed in gasps, holding their breath as long as possible, devoting their senses to listening. Chris looked up and was mortified. Large patches of blue sky broke through the leaves. "They're gonna see us!"

Chris' scalp tingled and his hair moved with a life of its own. He brushed the leaves away, but it continued. He placed his hand on his head and scratched.

"Ouch!" Something bit him.

He looked up. Ants swarmed off the branches like chocolate syrup, drenching his body in a fluid skin of armor. He watched in horror as the onslaught crawled over his face, up his nose, over his lips, down his shirt, into his underwear, and down his legs. He squirmed, crushing them. Pincers drove into his skin. He clenched his teeth. He didn't move. He didn't scream. He looked through the gaps in the leaves. The helicopter hovered directly above them. The swish-swish of its blades grew slower and louder as it dropped, swaying the branches and opening the gaps farther. He fought the current, gunning the throttle and cranking the steering wheel.

They must have spotted us.

Chris screamed. He couldn't remain silent. His body wasn't his anymore; the ants crawled into his ears. He imagined them inside his head, biting his brain. He swung the steering wheel right.

"Noo!" Michael yelled.

Chris looked into the whites of Michael's eyes. The ants swarmed into them. Michael closed them and yelled, "Wait, Chris!" The ants dove into his mouth. Michael clamped his lips tight and chewed.

Chris pulled the steering wheel back. *Oh God. I can't do this.*

The chopper blades grew quiet and disappeared.

Ten, nine, eight, seven, six, five, four, three, two, one.

"Agghhhh!"

Chris gunned the boat. Michael jumped over the edge, pulling his pants down and flashing his white bum before plunging into the river.

Chris stopped the engine and cannon-balled over the other side.

"Gah!"

He plunged into icy black. Shocked with cold, his lungs folded, pushing a plume of bubbles from his mouth. He closed his eyes and descended. His feet touched something soft, and he pulled his knees to his chest and popped open his eyes. Tanner's bloated body floated in front of him. Chris screamed, but with no air left, he choked. Tanner reached toward him and Chris pushed away, clawing and kicking his way toward the sun's rays.

"Pah!" He burst into warm air. Ants encircled him like an oil slick.

He stripped off his shirt and threw it into the boat. He ducked his head under, glanced through the water, terrified, stripped off his pants and underwear, and tossed them into the boat.

"Michael?"

"Yeah?"

"You all right?"

"Yeah."

Chris swam to the back of the boat. "Toss your clothes into the boat."

"Already have."

Chris clung to the ladder. His chattering teeth echoed against the polished surface.

Had he actually seen Tanner or had he imagined it?

He pulled himself into the boat to find Michael sitting naked in the passenger seat.

"A little shriveled, eh?" Chris chided.

"You're one to talk," Michael said. "At least I had some length to begin with."

Chris tugged open his pack and pulled Calomine lotion and cotton balls from the first aid kit.

"Here, put this on. It'll take the sting away."

Michael frowned. "It's pink. Are you kidding? Anyway, I'd have to bathe in it."

"Suck it up, Michael."

Chris grabbed his jeans and shook them, sending a cloud of ants into the air. He sat down, grabbed the Calomine lotion, soaked a cotton puff in it, and dabbed the pink liquid onto a bite mark on his stomach. "One."

"Michael, did you see anything strange in the water?"

"Nope. You were too far away. Why?"

"Funny." Chris shivered. "Nuthin'."

Chris lost track of time, but it felt like half an hour had passed.

Michael dabbed his knee. "Fifty eight, beat that."

Chris continued. "... 57, 58, 59, 60, 61, Hah!"

Michael grabbed his jeans. "You only win the unimportant stuff. Let's get dressed. I'd hate someone to see us like this. What time is it?"

"Just after six."

Chris pulled on his jeans and shirt, sat in the driver's seat, and started the motors.

CHAPTER 10

Michael stared into the sky. He thought there were stars, but they were faint and he wasn't sure. The motor hummed in waves, soft, then loud, then soft. He relaxed his muscles and exhaustion washed through his body. He felt sleepy and allowed his eyes to close. He spun like a top and plummeted into a black pit.

"Hmmmm."

The boat screamed into a dark tunnel. The roar glided over the water and reflected back with a delay, creating pulsations, like the wings of a butterfly. Michael looked at Chris. Chris stared forward, his eyes pinned with fear. Yellow eyes glimmered from the tunnel walls and reflected on the water's surface. It smelled like an open tin of tuna.

"What?"

Something black and crumpled floated on the water. It grew as they raced toward it. The pounding in Michael's chest accelerated.

It was dead.

Who's dead?

He felt it in his heart. He knew.

"No. Can't be," he whispered.

It rose from the surface. Green eyes, shimmering and sunk into a blue face, peered from under a dark hood.

She whispered. "Michael?"

He screamed. "Moaaaaaa!"

CHAPTER 11

Chris jumped, banging his knees under the dash.

Michael's lips were stretched over his teeth and they split as he screamed.

Chris grabbed Michael's arm and shook. "Michael! You're dreaming!"

Michael's eyes popped open and terror fled from them. "No! I'm not! She's dead! I saw her!"

"Saw who?"

"I think. I don't know, but she was dead and she called me."

"She called you? What? Your name?"

Michael started to shake. "Ye... yes, I think."

Chris patted Michael's shoulder. "Just a dream. Don't worry 'bout it."

The sun had dropped behind the mountains, grey monoliths with clouds clinging to their snow capped peaks like old man's hair. They looked ancient and angry. Black particles swarmed the air, chasing the last remnants of light away. Chris' arms erupted into goose flesh. The river was narrow, and he stared at the shore, fearful of running the boat into it. Chris pictured the map in his head. The river turned south before these mountains. They would have to leave the boat soon and cross the mountain range by foot.

Something changed. Did the river get louder? Chris wasn't sure. Perhaps his imagination. He backed off the throttle and stood to get a better view. The water seemed smoother. "Let's pull over and camp. All right?"

Chris rose off his seat. "What?"

The motor screamed. The river roared. His stomach leapt as though dropped from the Tower of Terror.

A sockeye salmon appeared from the sky, floated toward Michael, and slapped him across the face, lathering his mouth in slimy fish-goo. It landed in the boat, thrashing like a worm dug from the ground.

The boat pitched to the right. Chris swung the steering wheel left. "We're gonna die! We're gonna die!" He glanced back at a wall of water.

Waterfall! We went over a damn waterfall!

The boat slammed into water. Michael crashed into the windshield, splitting it in two. Chris' thigh cracked the steering wheel, shattering it into three pieces and spinning the boat around. It shot straight up and smashed onto its side. Chris fell out, grabbed the remains of the steering wheel as his head slapped the water, and pulled himself back in as the boat righted itself. He pushed the throttle and gunned the boat toward, as best he could tell, the shore. Pebbles fired through the jets and sprayed behind them like an avalanche. They screeched over forty feet of rocks and slammed into a tree.

Chris looked to his left. Michael stared at him, stunned, his mouth opening and closing like the gaping salmon. His eyebrow was cut. Blood rolled down his cheek and dripped onto his shirt.

"Yep, this'll do nicely," Chris said.

Chris hopped over his seat and stepped to the salmon. The fish, about two feet long with a hooked jaw and sharp teeth, flopped; its silver skin glittered in the dark. Chris threw himself down and pinned it to the floor, pulled it into his arms, hauled it over the boat, carried it to the river, and threw it in. He kneeled and splashed water over his hands and shirt, trying to wash off the fish goo.

"Gah! I stink like fish. Come on, Michael. Let's get the blood off your face and set up camp."

The boat rested under a cluster of poplar trees. Chris climbed in, fumbled through his backpack and pulled out a hatchet. He tripped out of the boat and fell onto the pebbled ground, driving rocks into his knees.

Bushes lay in clusters around them.

"I'll hack off branches, Michael. Toss them over the boat till it's covered."

"I can't see a thing."

"I know. Do your best."

Chris grabbed some branches and swung the blade into them. It slid off and struck a rock, splaying sparks onto his foot. He yanked on the branches, but they held tight and slid through his fingers.

"Shoot, missed."

He swung the axe again, and again, and the branches broke free. He passed them to Michael and grabbed another set.

Chris' hands hurt. He'd been hacking for an hour. "Are we done yet?"

"Yep. I think I covered the last spot. Where do you want the tent?"

"Closer to the river. There's sand down there."

Lighting flashed in the distance and the leaves on the trees broke into a dance.

"Hurry, Michael."

Stumbling in the dark, they set up the tent and threw their sleeping bags in as a wall of rain exploded on them. Chris crawled into his bag and lay on his back, shivering. He reached behind him and zipped up the door.

Lightning streaked.

"One one thousand, two one thousand, three..."

The thunder hit so hard the ground shook. Trees cracked and groaned like they were tearing their roots from the earth and running away.

Michael burst into tears. "I want to go home. I want this to end."

Chris sat up. "No, we have to. Mom and Dad."

"THEY WOULDN'T HAVE DONE THIS FOR US!"

Chris flinched. "Michael!"

"Would they? No way! Dad didn't even visit you at the hospital."

"Yeah, but you put me there."

"But nothing! Mom didn't even stick around. Did she?"

Chris was stunned. "Michael, you can't think like that. We have to get them. They're going to die."

"So what?" Michael screamed. His eyes glowed through the darkness.

Chris clenched his fists. *I'll punch his lights out!*

He grabbed Michael's shirt and swung at his head, connecting with Michael's mouth. His fingers stung against Michael's teeth and he gasped at how much it hurt.

Michael connected with Chris' ear sending a shock of pain through his head, followed by a punch into his lip. Chris tasted blood and had no time to raise his arms before five more blows struck his face and head. He threw his arms around Michael and pushed him into the ground. Moving his arm up, he wrapped it around Michael's throat and squeezed with all his might, gritting his teeth till they hurt. Michael squirmed under him and he squeezed harder.

"Stop! You're choking me." Michael was wheezing.

Chris wanted to choke Michael. He squeezed harder.

"Ssss, Stop!" Michael could barely squeal. Anger pushed Chris to the edge and he bore down harder.

Michael stopped squirming.

"What are you doing?" Chris whispered. He dropped Michael, and he hit the ground with a thud.

"Michael, are you?" Chris felt around for him. Michael wasn't moving. Numbness spread through Chris' hands and they started to shake. Had he killed his own brother?

Michael coughed and burst into tears.

Chris wrapped his arms around him. "Jeez, Michael. I'm sorry. I didn't mean to."

Michael wailed. "I can't do this anymore, Chris. I'm scared! I need, I need Mom. I wanna go home!"

"Sshhh, it's all right. We'll find them," Chris said.

The tent collapsed onto Chris' face and billowed out with a slap. He levitated as a gust of wind forced itself under and pushed them up like a kite.

Michael wailed louder.

Chris had held Michael for an hour, and Michael slept with irregular breaths. Chris had never seen Michael lose it like that. He'd never seen Michael scared until yesterday. He'd never hit Michael until tonight. It was a week of firsts.

The weight of responsibility was crushing. His eyeballs, ears, and temples were assaulted with waves of pain.

Damn you, Dad. Damn you, Mom. Why did you do this? What the heck are you involved in?

Lighting flashed.

"One one thous..."

Thunder exploded and the tent walls billowed.

Chris prayed for sleep.

"What do you mean, you didn't find them?" The phone crackled under the force of Kuma's screaming.

"All we found was a life preserver."

"Where?"

"In the tributary. It runs alongside their home on the opposite side of the river."

"Did you cover the whole river?"

"Mainly east of the house. We did a quick fly-over west but didn't spend much time there. They did head east."

"No, they didn't, you idiot!"

"B-but, we saw them!"

"Did you see them in the tributary?"

"No."

"Damn brats! They doubled back you fool! Start again. Head west. I want every square inch covered, all the way to the mountains!"

"Yes, sir!

CHAPTER 12

The tent lay still and glowed like a lamp, but something roared outside.

Chris' brain felt like an ice pack, and his muscles and bones ached with cold. If he moved, they would snap in two, like a Popsicle slammed into a counter. Was he dead? He tried to lift his arm but couldn't. He tried to close his eyes, but they wouldn't. No, he must be somewhere between awake and asleep. This had happened to him before, seeing and hearing all around him while in a dream. He found, through practice, he could wake himself by making a noise. He tried to yell, but his voice stuck. He breathed deeply and pushed air through his vocal cords, clamping them to produce a sound of any kind. A squeak rose from his lips. He pushed harder. The squeak rose to a scream and the scream hurled him from sleep. He threw out his arm, plunging it into ice water, and flopped onto his side.

"Whah? Michael?" Chris felt the lump on his head and remembered the fight. Did Michael crawl away? What if he got lost or drowned? "No, Michael!"

Chris jumped onto his knees and wrestled the sodden sleeping bag off, peeling it over his feet and tossing it aside. He zipped open the mosquito netting and peeked out. The river had gone wild, spilling onto the beach and pouring through their tent. A tree trunk crashed over the waterfall, spun around, and vanished into a whirlpool.

He crawled outside. The current tugged at his feet and he staggered and stepped on a sharp rock, slicing his foot with immense pain, even through his frozen flesh.

He looked around, but couldn't see Michael. "Michael!"

The thunderous roar of the falls hijacked Chris' voice. He hugged himself to stop shivering, which forced the shaking to his legs and made it worse.

He grabbed the tent and pulled, but it pulled back and he stumbled and fell. Laden with water, it must have weighed hundreds of pounds. Slinging the material over his shoulder, he turned toward the shore, leaned forward, dragged it just clear of the water, and collapsed to the ground, panting.

Tears stung his eyes, and he wiped them away, embarrassed by his need to cry. From the day Michael was born he'd vowed to protect his little brother and for once, given the chance, he'd failed. Michael had probably drowned or wandered away and died of hyperthermia. Chris beat the sand with his fist. "Damn you! Why? Why us?"

His thoughts broken by his clattering teeth, he crawled to the boat and pulled himself inside. Rummaging through his backpack he pulled out matches and dry newspaper and, hopping out of the boat, found some twigs on the ground. They felt greasy and damp.

He scrunched the newspaper up and struck a match. A flame flared. The wind snuffed it out. He grabbed another match and struck it, shielding it with his hand. He pushed it into the newspaper, but his hand shook so hard he couldn't keep the flame on it.

"Damn!" Smoke curled from the match. He pulled out another match and tried again, pushing all his energy, his life, into his hand. "Stop shaking."

A flame grew from the newspaper. He smiled. The paper burned fast, curling into a smoldering pile. Chris grabbed the sticks and threw them on, but they smothered the flames into a ball of smoke. He darted around like a hungry chipmunk, looking for dry grass and tossing it onto the charcoaled paper.

"Where's Michael? Just when I need him most."

The wet grass smothered the flames and white smoke billowed from the wreckage.

His breathing turned choppy and sporadic.

Michael must be as cold.

He wanted to lie down on the stones, steaming in the morning sun, and go to sleep.

He shuffled into the bushes and pulled up dry grass, protected from the rain by the foliage above. After five minutes he had a large pile. His muscles warmed from the activity, giving him strength. He pushed into the bushes and found dry, broken twigs and dead branches. He gathered an armful and tossed them into a mound by the grass. He crumpled three sheets of newspaper into round balls and piled some of the grass onto the newspaper, but not so much that it would snuff out the flame. He lit a match, protecting it from the wind with cupped hands, and lit the newspaper, gently setting the grass on top. The flames roared through the grass and jumped six inches from the ground. He added more grass, then twigs, followed by more grass, then the bigger sticks. Soon, the fire reached his knees. Feeling proud, he stood over the flames and rubbed his hands. He jeans grew warm, and steam curled from them.

Chris glanced around. The river was lined with a sand bank about forty feet in width, which blended into a line of rocks like an esker, each round like a bowling ball. Following the rocks lay a thick swath of green birch trees within a carpet of tall, green grass. A steep hill lay behind the trees but with his view blocked by the treetops, he couldn't see how high it went. Michael could have gone in any direction.

A tree shook. Chris froze.

Michael popped from the forest with a huge grin.

He's alive! Chris thought. But why did he look so happy? Chris shook his head. He shouted, "Where the heck have you been?"

"Searchin'. You look cold."

"Of course I'm cold." Chris clenched his fists. "I've been running around here trying to save our butts and you've been out picking daisies!" Chris turned to the fire and rubbed his hands over the flames. He smiled in spite of his anger, relieved his brother was alive. Something was odd. He looked back at Michael. "You're dry? What the...?"

"Follow me," Michael said, turning back toward the trees.

Chris ran after him. They trudged through the forest to the hill. It was steep and as tall as the trees, and Chris groaned. Michael jumped into the bank and slid back with an avalanche of sand. "It's hard work, Chris."

Chris pushed himself over the top, lay in the grass, and listened to them pant. "Sound like a couple of Chihuahuas." He grinned and dragged himself up. "Huh?"

A red wall towered above him. "What's this?" His ear lobes

prickled.

"This way." Michael jumped up and dashed alongside the barn wall. He reached a door at the far end and opened it. "Its got a wood stove. Take your clothes off and drape them over."

"You've been sitting here warming your tush while I've been running around trying to light a dinky fire?" Chris sputtered.

"Not my fault I'm the smarter one."

Chris' throat constricted. He gurgled and started to pace, hoping to calm his shaking legs.

The floor was dirt and covered in old hay. Two logs, dug into the ground, towered up and offered support to thousands of pounds of thick beams that held the roof far above their heads. A second floor covered the southern half of the barn. Chris climbed a handmade ladder up to it.

A stack of hay bales, neatly interconnected, covered the floor to the back wall. The walls and roof were constructed with tightly placed 2x6 planks. A single window on the south wall flooded the second floor with light.

Chris climbed down and peered into the horse stalls, enclosed with black iron gates and lining the east wall. They were empty. The west wall held rakes, shovels, hoes, axes, chains, a sink with running water, pulleys, saddles, and tools Chris couldn't identify.

The iron stove sat by the north wall, its vent stack directed up and out behind it. A pen in the northwest corner enclosed with a swinging gate and plywood contained a few dozen fluffy chicks.

Michael walked over to him. "Do you think they torture people here?"

Chris glanced at the scars in the beams. "Dunno. Should we wait to find out?"

"You bet! We can drag our stuff in, dry it out, and hide in the mezzanine, and there's baby chicks in case we get hungry."

Chris rubbed his tummy. "Hmmm, Kentucky Fried Chicks."

Michael laughed and turned toward the door. "There's a house down the road and another barn, and a vegetable garden. There must be a thousand acres of corn. We can bake it on the stove."

Chris trudged after him. "Well then, let's get our stuff, I guess."

Chris dug his fingers into the sand. His foot slipped. He clawed and slid into Michael, knocking him over and onto his back. Michael groaned.

"Sorry, Michael. Last trip."

Each load felt heavier. Chris thought it would take an hour to carry the stuff up the hill. Two hours had passed since they had started. The tent and sleeping bags hung like corpses from the trees. They would dry soon if the breeze kept up. He clambered over the hill, into the barn, and up the ladder.

They dragged hay bales into a row along the front of the mezzanine and tossed their stuff behind it.

Chris climbed down the ladder and looked up. "Perfectly hidden."

Michael dashed out the door to steal some corn. Chris tore open a package of KD, tossed it into a pot of water, and placed it on the stove.

"I wonder who owns this place?" Michael asked through a mouthful of corn.

Chris rubbed his mouth with the back of his hand and smacked his lips. "Dunno, but I'm sure we'll meet them before nightfall. They must check on the chicks. We better get our stuff off the trees and clean this place up."

Michael grabbed another cob. "Hmmm, one more piece."

It was 4:00PM. Chris burped and weaved to the ladder while rubbing his tummy. Michael wiggled into his sleeping bags. "I'll keep watch," Chris said. He crawled into his sleeping bag and leaned onto a hay bale. Sunbeams pierced cracks in the walls, illuminating dust particles. Dancing and swirling like gold dust, they blanketed Chris with millions of bright apparitions. Aliens, he thought with a grin. He could hear flies, thousands of them. They laced into Michael's breaths with a monotonous buzz.

He remembered no more.

CHAPTER 13

Michael popped out of a dreamless sleep and stared into the barn roof. The wood slats, laid parallel like an airport runway, pulled his gaze to the barn wall and down to the window. The poplar trees swayed with the wind. Recognizing his surroundings, he rolled over, grabbed Chris' wrist, and checked the time. It was 9:00AM. He sure missed his cell. He couldn't tell time, text his friends, or play games.

"We slept for seventeen hours?"

He heard a scrunching noise like someone walking on popcorn. His nylon sleeping bag was soaked with sweat and stuck to his legs. He peeled it off, tugged on his jeans, and crawled over the block of hay beside him. The straw poked his arms and flicked dust into his nose.

"Ah-choo!"

He wiped his nose and peered over the edge. "Nothin' there."

He turned, faced the ladder, and set his foot on the first rung. His muscles burned against the stretch, a painful reminder of their day from hell. He pushed on until his feet touched the soft floor. He limped to the stove, tossed in a log, and rubbed his hands above the warmth, sighing with satisfaction.

He heard the noise again and glanced at the door. Was it coming from outside? His heart thumping, he swung around and scanned the barn.

The chicks? No, maybe a horse?

He sauntered to the door and reached for the handle, but it swung open on its own. He gasped. Numbness spread through his arms, legs, and hands. He tried to swallow, but it lodged in his throat like a balloon. "Thomas?"

Thomas gaped at Michael as though his sanctuary, the one place in the world he felt safe, had been breached by the devil. His pupils ballooned, pushing his grey irises to a thin band and revealing black windows leading to the depths of fury.

Thomas grabbed a hoe at the side of the door and thwacked it into Michael's skull. The pain was so intense Michael froze and watched the vibrations race up the handle, through Thomas' arms, and into his soul.

"Uh-oh," Michael said.

Thomas swung the hoe again. Michael collapsed to the floor and curled into a ball, squeezing his eyes closed against a river of tears.

"You jerk," Thomas screamed. Michael felt the hoe hit the side of his head. Did his ear fall off? He bit his cheek.

"Get out of my life!" The hoe thumped into Michael's chest and he yelped at the pain. Black dots circled his eyes, and he had a flashback of kicking Thomas in the stomach as he lay on the street, crying.

"I hate you!" The hoe cracked into Michael's skull, and he started to fall down a dark well.

"Thomas! Stop!"

A girl's voice? Who was that? Michael felt the hoe hit the side of his neck, and he fell into black...

CHAPTER 14

Chris bolted out of his sleeping bag and over the hay bale in one leap. He hit the ladder and wash-boarded down it, hitting the ground with a thud. A bolt of pain shot through his knees and triggered a tortuous back spasm. He wiped tears from his eyes and scanned the barn.

Michael lay still on the ground and Thomas, crumpled in a heap, cried like his pet dog had died. An angel, dressed in blue jeans and a white blouse, the most beautiful girl Chris had ever seen, watched the melee with a look of bewilderment.

"Thomas?" Chris whimpered.

The girl dashed to Michael. Bending down beside him, she thrust her fingers under his neck and placed her cheek at his mouth.

"Oh, thank God," she said. "He's still alive."

She looked up at Chris and her eyes were like icicles. "You. Whoever you are!" she yelled. "Get a blanket, now!"

Chris turned and dashed up the ladder. He grabbed his sleeping bag, a pot, a towel, some water, and a first aid kit and hopped down. "Here," he said, throwing the sleeping bag to the girl. He poured water into the pot, slapped it onto the stove, and tossed in a log. Closing the stove door, he turned to look at Thomas. He was sitting against the wall, his legs up against his chest and folded into his arms. He stared at Michael, and his lip seemed curled like he'd just eaten overcooked broccoli. The girl was leaning over Michael and staring into his face.

"What now?" Chris asked.

The girl looked at him, and her jaw hardened, like she was holding back a laugh. "You can start by putting your pants on."

Chris froze. He'd had dreams like this. He looked at his hairy legs. Covered in pink polka dot Calamine lotion, they looked ridiculous against his red underwear. His face prickled.

"Uh, yeah. I'll be right back."

He crawled up the ladder and grabbed his jeans. Who was she? His legs were shaking, and he struggled to get his pant legs over his feet. He pulled on his T-shirt and stepped down the ladder. The girl was still sitting with Michael, and Thomas was leaning against the barn wall staring into nothing.

"How is he?" Chris asked.

"Fine. His airway's clear and he's breathing." She looked into Chris' eyes. "Who are you?" Her voice wavered.

Chris' mouth moved but made no sound. His heart pounded against his temples. His cheeks turned warm and prickly and his ear lobes tickled. The odor of hay, dirt, smoke, baby chicks, wood, and sweat intensified, flooding his olfactory senses with a bang. He blinked and stared.

Brilliant red hair flowed over her shoulders. Ice blue eyes lit up the freckles on her cheeks, accenting a fine, reserved nose and lips that even when angry formed a smile. Dimples appeared at the corners of her mouth when she frowned, and her eyes sparkled with an intense mix of fury and empathy.

Chris realized he was looking at her lips and thinking about kissing her. He blushed and turned away. "Later. Don't worry. I'll take Michael if you want to check on Thomas.

"By the way, my name is Chris. I'm Michael's brother. He's the guy bleeding all over the ground."

She cracked a grin and blushed. "I'm Katherine. Thomas is my brother."

Behind his curtain of hair, Chris could feel her piercing gaze. His heart pounded, forcing the extra blood supply demanded by his organs.

"Holy! You're those two boys! You're on the news."

Chris' head shot up. He looked right at her.

"Like I said, we'll talk later."

"I'm so sorry about this," Katherine whispered.

"Don't worry, Michael deserved it."

Katherine glared at Chris. Her cheeks glowed. "Pardon?"

"Never mind. Later."

Chris squirted dish soap into the steaming water and dipped in the towel, wringing the scalding water out with his fingertips. Michael was in the exact position he should be, lying on his side with his head on his arm. Chris sat beside Michael and listened for his breathing, which sounded peaceful, and at that moment wondered if Michael would come back again.

Chris looked at Katherine. "I'm glad Thomas grabbed the wrong end of the hoe."

She cringed. "Yeah, I doubt Michael would have lived if Thomas hit him with the metal part."

Chris wiped away the blood, revealing a laceration that almost cut Michael's ear lobe in half. There were four lumps on Michael's head, bruised but not bleeding. He had a black eye and a purple bruise that covered his neck. Chris applied antibiotic cream to Michael's ear and pulled the flesh together with a butterfly bandage. He left the other wounds to air.

Katherine sat beside Thomas, pulled him onto her lap, and rocked him. He started to cry, rippling his emotions through the barn like a pebble dropped into a pond, fear, hurt, pity, and embarrassment. Chris absorbed them like a tuning fork. He squeezed his eyes, but tears pushed through.

Chris hated his brother.

Punches, kicks, and name calling flashed through Chris' mind. He relived the darkest corners of his life. He relived the terror of his Mom and Dad's kidnapping. He relived the day a gang of kids trapped him in the corner between the school gym and art room and punched him until he passed out. He relived his disappointment the day he found out Michael became the leader of that gang.

He blubbered and wailed against an onslaught of anger and embarrassment. Katherine would never look at him again. He was an idiot.

Chris didn't know how long he'd been crying but he felt better. An ant scuttled through the straw littering the barn floor and crawled onto his shoe lace.

"Chris," Katherine said.

"Uh-huh."

"Your brother's been out for five minutes. I should get my

grandparents to check him."

Chris flicked the ant off his lace. "Uh, I don't know. That might be a bad idea."

"Worse than him dying of a concussion?" Her lips pressed into a tight line.

"Actually, that may not be a bad thing..." His voice trailed as she glared at him.

Michael bolted up and rubbed the back of his neck. His eyeballs spun as though he was possessed. "Gah, bet that was worse than the gopher snake."

Katherine raised her eyebrows. "Snake? The news said it was a gopher. I wondered how a gopher could reach his testicles"

Chris jumped to his feet. "Enough!"

"Of course, I don't know how a snake could reach your testicles either," Katherine said while eyeing Chris' height.

Chris glared at her. His cheeks prickled. He needed to scratch them but resisted. He looked at Michael. "You okay?"

"No, head hurts."

"I need some answers," Katherine said. "What's going on, Michael – between you and Thomas?"

Michael looked down.

"Michael," Chris demanded, "give it up."

"I've been a jerk," Michael mumbled. "I lead a gang of kids at school. We..."

"What did I ever do to you?" Thomas asked. His voice quivered.

Michael squirmed. "Nothing, it was me."

"Beat up yourself then."

"Michael?" Katherine said. "What did you do to my brother?"

Tears fell from Michael's cheeks. "I...we, we chased him down, after school."

Katherine's eyes hardened. "When?"

"All...all the time."

"Why? He's just a little kid."

Michael lifted his head and looked at her. "I deserved it, what I got today."

Katherine glared at him. "Yeah, I think you did."

Thomas looked at Michael. "When you get back to school I want you to shut that gang down. No kid will go through what I did."

A gust of wind rustled the leaves outside. The river's gurgling grew louder.

Katherine stared at Chris. Thomas eyed Michael like a rabbit watching a wolf. Chris dropped his head from Katherine's gaze and traced the blue stitching through his sneakers.

"Chris, what's going on? Why are you guys running from the police?" Katherine asked.

The rustling stopped. An Osprey called in the distance.

Chris sat down. "Our parents were kidnapped."

Chris cursed under his breath. He shouldn't say anything, but the admission lifted him and cracked the fear, rage, and despair suppressed in the pit of his stomach. He continued. The words created the story. He became an observer, no longer telling but listening. The sun passed over the roof and breached the cracks in the west wall. The razor thin beams warmed his back. He looked up, realizing the words had stopped; the story finished. He glanced at Katherine. Her mouth hung open and she stared at him.

Chris fidgeted. Say something, he thought. Crap, she doesn't believe me.

"Chris…that's incredible." A tear rolled down her cheek. "I can't imagine what you…"

Katherine gazed into Chris' eyes. He locked on, unable to tear away. His hands became cold and sweaty.

"Is there anything I can do?" She asked.

"I'll take a hug," Chris mumbled.

He dropped his head in horror. *Where did that come from?*

"Pardon?"

"Nuh, nothing. Nothing for now. We need to rest. Do you mind if we stay for awhile?"

Katherine's eyes lit up. "No problem. My grandparents will be happy to feed you."

"No!" Chris said. "They can't know we're here!"

She looked down. "Oh, sorry. What about the police?"

"No. They wouldn't believe us anyway."

"Oh."

"By the way, why haven't I met you?" Chris asked.

"I go to James Dingwall High School on the north side of town."

"Isn't that a school for geniuses?"

She laughed. "No, not geniuses. Just higher than average marks."

"Oh, do you have a boyfriend?"

N.D. RICHMAN

Katherine giggled. "No, I don't. And what's it to you?"

"Couldn't help myself." Chris' voice trailed off. Her giggle was like a well. He fell into it.

Katherine stood. "We'd better go. Grandma and Grandpa will be worried. Do you guys know how to play Rummy?"

"You bet," Chris said.

"Or at least I did before my brains were beaten out," Michael said.

"Great. I'll bring a deck of cards."

"I'll hide the hoe," Michael said.

Katherine turned to Chris. "We'll bring food."

"Thanks, Katherine," Chris said. He pushed the door closed.

"Do you have a boyfriend?" Michael repeated in a whiny voice. He laughed and rolled onto his back. "Ow-ow-ow geez, that hurts!"

"Wait right there. I'm gonna get the chains," Chris said.

Michael flopped onto his stomach and groaned. "Just kidding. Let me know when the food gets here. I'm starving."

Chris opened the door and peeked outside. The afternoon sun reflected off the red barn walls, disfiguring the air with waves of heat. He watched Katherine and Thomas walk down the dirt road toward their home. She stopped, leaned down to Thomas' height, and talked to him. She gave him a hug. Chris felt a twinge of guilt, watching their moment. He dashed to the north side of the barn to an open patch of grass and lay in it and grinned, pleased with his hiding spot. He stared at the sky and thought about her, her voice, her eyes, her hair, her dimples; even her lime green nail polish. He didn't know what to do; approach her or hide. Katherine was way too pretty for him, the kind of girl he'd slink away from for fear of being rejected. Maybe he should just go for it. But why was he thinking about her anyway? His parents were in mortal danger, and so were they. He frowned.

Chris heard two sets of footsteps crunching in the gravel. One dragged like a crust of bread scraped over a cheese grater, the other crisp and confident. Had he fallen asleep? He stood and waved at Thomas and Katherine. Katherine lugged a wicker basket. Thomas smiled and waved back.

As they approached, Chris ran to the barn door, opened it, and yelled at Michael, "Get up!"

Michael lifted his head and plopped it back into the hay. "Gah!"

74

Chris walked to him and nudged his shoulder. "What?"

"My head, ohhh, it's gonna explode."

Chris heard Katherine behind him. "Tylenol?" she asked.

"Yeah," Chris said. "You brought some?"

Katherine placed the basket in front of the stove, pulled out a bottle of Tylenol, and tossed it to Chris. "Extra strength. Give him a couple. Come on, Michael. Food will make you feel better." She pulled out two plates, each with a hamburger and cob of corn, and tore off the cellophane. Michael staggered over and took one. She passed the other to Chris. "I've got chocolate cake, too," she said.

Chris stared at the hamburger. The sesame seeds looked like bullets. The ketchup drooled like blood. He pressed his lips together and clenched his teeth. He stopped the tears but not the wobble in his chin.

"You all right, Chris?" Katherine asked.

"Yeah. I haven't seen a hot meal in two days."

Chris crunched into the corn. The kernels exploded onto his tongue like machine gun fire. The butter was fresh and creamy. He forced the corn past the lump in his throat and wiped his trembling chin with the back of his hand. His mouth watered. He heaved, almost bringing it back up. He looked down, behind his wall of hair, to avoid Katherine's gaze.

"Let's play," Katherine said. She grabbed a deck of cards from the basket, sat down, and started to shuffle them.

Chris put his plate down and sat beside her. Michael and Thomas sat, forming a circle.

"Why do gorillas have big nostrils?" Thomas asked while Katherine passed out the cards.

"Dunno," Chris replied.

"'Cause they have big fingers."

Chris burst into laughter, flopped down, and rolled over. He tried to stop laughing and snorted.

Michael started laughing. "Ow-ow-ow." He fell on his back, grabbed his sides, and squealed. He farted.

Chris kicked his feet and roared. "Need, oxygen."

Thomas giggled and squealed.

Chris swallowed his laughter and glanced at Katherine through teared eyes. She stared at him with her mouth hung open. Chris thought of the salmon gaping for air and laughed harder.

Katherine shook her head. "You guys are nuts. Let's play."

"All right," Chris said. He sat up and took a big bite from his burger.

Chris' knees bounced. He won the last two games and was one card from going out. He picked up a card from the stack, an ace of hearts. He tossed the card onto the ground. "Just what I needed. I'm out."

"Again?" Michael whined.

Katherine gathered the cards. "Come on, Thomas, we better go." She grabbed the basket, shooed Thomas through the door, and stopped. "Chris?"

Chris hopped up, puffed his chest, and swaggered toward her. His heart tripped over its beats. His knees threatened to buckle. He gazed into her eyes as he approached. "Yes?" he asked, deepening his voice.

"You stink."

Chris gaped. "Oh. Uh, thanks?"

Katherine giggled.

Her face lit up like a crimson sunset when she giggled.

"No. I, I meant your clothes. I can put them in the washer, if you wish. I'll sneak them back tonight when they're dry."

"Oh, yeah, please. I'd like that. We'll change into our swimming trunks."

"I'll wait," Katherine said.

"You don't want to wash our underwear, do you?"

"I'm afraid I should, from what I saw of them." She grinned.

Chris' head flushed. "Ah yeah, okay."

Chris turned and plodded to Michael. Grabbing Michael's arm, he herded him toward the ladder.

"What?" Michael asked.

"She wants our clothes."

"Whoh, Chris."

"No, no, you twit! Don't be gross. She's offered to clean them for us. Get your swimming trunks on."

"She's gonna see our underwear?"

"Don't be a baby, Michael."

After he pulled on his trunks Chris swept up the clothes and carried them down. He dropped them into the basket. "Thanks, Katherine."

"No problem. Oh, one more thing." She rummaged through the basket. "I brought some soap and shampoo. There's a big aluminum wash tub in the corner. Fill it with hot water and scrub down. You'll want to finish before I get back."

"Uh, yeah, we'll finish before you get back." Chris closed the door. *Brilliant, the words just flow.*

Chris tossed the last bucket of dirty bath water into the trees. They had to boil the water on the stove, and it took over an hour for them to bathe. He grinned, thinking about the wash tub. He plopped his bum in, but his legs and arms wouldn't fit and he had to leave them draped over the sides. Michael howled so hard he fell over. It felt good to be clean, though, and Katherine might get a little closer, now that he wasn't covered in sweat-laden dirt and fish slime.

"Why don't you get some sleep," he said to Michael as he walked into the barn. "I'll stay down here for a bit."

"And miss you making a fool of yourself in front of Katherine?"

"Go to bed, Michael."

Michael put his hands on his hips and glared at him. "You're playing boss again."

Chris threw down the bucket and it bounced up, hitting him in his stomach. Michael smirked, which made him madder. "It's about time I played boss, dammit! Cut it. You're tired. Go!"

Michael clenched his fists, but then his shoulders dropped, and Chris sensed defeat. He limped toward the ladder, mumbling, and heaved himself up.

"Michael?"

Michael stopped and looked around.

"Do you get it now?" Chris asked.

"Get what?"

"What you did? To Thomas? And the rest?"

Michael dropped his gaze to the floor. "Yeah, I get it."

"Won't happen again?"

Michael turned around and stepped up the ladder. "No."

Chris gathered the map and spread it on the ground. He heard footsteps outside.

"Chris?" Katherine called, "Are you decent?"

Chris jumped up. "I've got my trunks on."

"Great. Let me know when you're decent then."

Chris grinned and opened the door.

Katherine glided in. Did her feet touch the ground?

"What's that?" she asked while looking down at the map.

"Our route."

"Can you show me?"

"You bet. Can I get my clothes on first?"

"Those swimming trunks are a little hard to look at."

"Oh." *What?* "Sure."

Katherine sat on the ground in front of the map. She placed two mugs beside her and opened a thermos. "I brought hot chocolate."

Chris dashed into a horse stall and crouched down. He fumbled his underwear and dropped them. "Shoot, settle down." He pulled them on backwards. A piece of straw stabbed his bum. "Chris you're an idiot!" he whispered.

"Wow," Katherine said, "you guys are hiking over the mountains?"

"Uh-huh." Chris squirmed as he walked, scratched his bum, and sat beside her.

His heart pounded. A blush swarmed his face. He dropped his head. *She smells like strawberries.*

"Coruntan, on the other side. We need to get there."

"Yeah, but the mountains, they're huge."

"Yep. We'll avoid the peaks, shouldn't have to top three-thousand feet."

Katherine looked up at him. "It's a long way."

"Twenty miles to the mountains, forty miles over. We're staying here for the night." Chris pointed to a spot on the map.

"Natalia Lake. I hear it's beautiful," Katherine said. "Sits in a valley. It's fed from a glacier."

"Nice," Chris said. "There's a river flowing out both sides. We're going to follow it to the ocean."

"How big is Coruntan?" Katherine asked.

"Two million plus, bigger than any city I've ever seen before. We'll cross twenty miles of it to reach the ocean."

"What then?"

"Robert's island. It's this one, right here."

"Wow. How'll you get across?"

"Don't know. We're working on that. The island is supposed to be a guarded fortress."

"How long for the trip?"

"Three days across the mountains, another day to the island. We have to leave in the morning."

"Chris, you should stay another day. Michael is beat up and your supplies are low."

"But we've only got ..."

"I don't care what you've got. Let's sit down tomorrow and figure out what you need. We can stock you up."

Chris stared at the map. "I'd like to, but Kuma said he'd kill our parents in two weeks. We're going to arrive just in time, at best, assuming they're even there."

"Chris, what if we saddled a couple of horses for you? Thomas and I can ride with you to the mountains. I'll tell Grandma and Grandpa we're going on a day ride. That'll knock some time off your trip, and you can stay and rest tomorrow."

"You'd do that? "

"Of course."

"I, yeah. That would be great. But I, we...we've never ridden a horse before."

"In that case, you won't be thanking me. Be prepared for a sore butt." She giggled. "There's a trail," Katherine said.

"Where?"

"I think it follows the river. People ride horses to Natalia Lake. I bet there's a path down the other side."

"I wasn't looking forward to bushwhacking."

"And Michael?" Katherine asked.

"A techno geek. Not much into the outdoors. How's Thomas?"

"Pretty upset. Though relieved, I think. Bashing Michael did him good."

"Stress relieving dummy, should rent him out," Chris said.

Katherine giggled for a second. Then her eyes flared and Chris could feel the anger strike out. "I had no idea what he was doing to Thomas. Why didn't Thomas tell me?"

Chris looked down. "I've always been angry with Michael. But it's strange. There's a whole side to him I didn't even know existed. I thought he was an idiot, but he's a damn genius. You wouldn't believe what he's capable of, and he's just been wasting it."

Katherine gulped her hot chocolate and stood. "I better get back."

Chris jumped up and looked at the floor. "Thanks, Katherine."

Katherine wrapped her arms around his waist and pulled him in. Chris circled his arms around her back and squeezed. He ran his fingers along her shoulder blade. Her back muscles bulged under her skin, forming ridges and valleys. He followed them down, buried his head into her hair, and laid his cheek on her neck. She felt strong, yet inviting. A lump rose in his throat.

I'll remember that strawberry shampoo for the rest of my life.

Katherine released her hold. "I'll see you in the morning after we've finished our chores."

Chris squeezed tight. "You bet."

He swept the hair from his eyes, held his head high, and smiled.

She grinned. "You've got really nice eyes when you show them." She slipped out the door.

He looked up into the wood beams and sighed. He felt he would burst, as though a lifetime of happiness was squished into his heart. "Yep, I'm gonna blow."

Chris slipped into his sleeping bag, placed his head onto the prickly hay, and listened to the beetles crawl under him. He couldn't sleep. He had spent a lifetime without his parents. Why did he miss them so much now?

CHAPTER 15

Chris plopped onto the ground and wiped the sweat off his forehead. It had taken an hour to dump their belongings, make a list of missing items, and pack them again.

Michael scurried around like a Walmart shopper.

"Whatcha doing?" Chris asked.

"Makin' a chick feeder."

Michael grabbed the gidgit bag and pulled some objects out, each about the size of his hand. He placed them on the ground.

"What are those?" Chris asked.

"A timer, AC adaptor, a motor, a rubber band."

"Oh."

Michael climbed the ladder and disappeared, returning with a fertilizer spreader, a green bucket with a long handle, an eraser sized hole on the bottom, rubber wheels, and a white disk under the bucket. As he approached, Michael grabbed a wheel and turned it, and the disk spun. "I saw this up there last night. The wheels are connected to the disk and this feeder inside." Michael pointed to a spaghetti width metal rod inside the bucket which spun like a popcorn machine mixer. "As you push the spreader, the fertilizer is fed through the hole and onto the disk, which flings it over the grass."

Chris shook his head. "Why, Michael?"

Michael dropped to his knees and grabbed a crescent wrench. "Why what?"

"You, you can hack computers, wire lights, set up cameras, and now build chick feeders out of nothing. Why pretend to be so stupid and mean?"

Michael set the wrench on a wheel bolt, then took it off and looked at Chris. He glanced down at the ground. "Being mean and stupid feels more…like me, I guess."

"But, imagine what people could have thought of you."

"I don't care what people think of me. No one would have noticed anyway. I'm done with the stupid talk. Can you help me?"

Chris got up and held the spreader as Michael removed the wheels and handle. "What now?" Chris asked.

Michael pointed to the wall above the chick pen. "Hold it onto the wall and I'll bolt it on."

The spreader now hanging on the wall, Michael mounted the motor, timer, and adaptor and connected them with some red wire he pulled out of the bag, and placed a thick rubber band from the motor rotor to the fertilizer spreader shaft. He plugged it in. The motor spun the disk.

"Looks good," Chris said.

Michael turned and scanned the barn. "Now, chick feed."

Chris pointed to the horse stall beside the chicks. "There's a bag of it in there."

Michael disappeared inside and walked out with an old ice cream bucket full of food. He poured it into the feeder and fiddled with the timer. The disk spun, throwing food around the pen, and stopped.

"I set it for two feeds a day," Michael explained.

Chris grinned. "Cool. Was there fertilizer left in the spreader?"

Michael frowned. "Hmm, didn't think of that. Maybe they'll grow real big."

The barn door banged open and Chris spun around, his heart pounding against his chest. Katherine strode through the barn door, her face flush and eyes bright. Thomas, bouncing like a gazelle, followed.

"Hi, guys!" she called.

"Jeez. Can you guys knock?" Chris asked. He pulled the list from his pocket and walked toward her. "It's all here. We need food, and Michael hogged the medical supplies."

Michael threw a role of electrical tape at Chris. "Funny, Chris."

Thomas grabbed the list and skipped out of the barn.

"He's a little happier, eh?" Chris asked.

"Been like this all morning," Katherine replied. "Driving me nuts. I better go help him."

The barn door hit the wall like a gunshot.

Chris jumped. "I'll kill 'em."

Thomas strode in, carrying two blue woolen sweaters and a coil of red rope. Katherine followed, carrying a box of food. Thomas dropped the rope with a grunt. It hit the ground with a thud, raising a plume of dust.

Michael nodded toward the sweaters. "What's with those?"

"Gets cold in the mountains," Thomas said.

"And the rope?"

"You'll need to raise your backpacks into the trees."

"Why?"

"Keep the bears from your food."

Michael frowned. "Oh."

Thomas' eyes danced. He grinned.

"No worries," Chris said. "Just keep your food out of the tent."

Michael leapt to his feet and walked to Thomas. Thomas jumped, as though deflecting a punch.

"Come on," Chris said. "Let's get that stuff into the packs."

Michael dashed over to Chris and leaned toward him. "See?" he whispered.

"What?" Chris asked.

"I'm trying to be nice and he's still scared of me."

"Nice? What have you done to be nice?"

Michael frowned. "I haven't punched him, for one. This is hard. It was easier being a jerk."

"Huh?"

"Now I spend more time worrying about Thomas than myself."

Chris grinned. "Nice to see you with the rest of us, kind of. It's hard, but worth it."

"Yeah, I'm just surprised. I thought it would be easier."

"You truly appreciate the things you work for," Chris said.

Michael's jaw dropped. "What? You're Confucius now?"

Chris grinned. "Come on. Let's get these things ready."

The backpacks filled, Chris and Katherine sat on the ground, watching Michael show Thomas the chick feeder.

"Hey, guys. This is cool," Thomas called.

Katherine jumped up and bolted to the door.

Chris swung around as she dashed out of the barn. "Wha…?"

Katherine yelled, "Can't catch me!"

Thomas and Michael ran after her. Chris scrambled up and blew through the door. Thomas disappeared around the north corner. Chris sprinted after him. He flew past Thomas, bore down on Michael, and blew by him as they reached the trees. Chris leapt over a log and bounded through the forest. Katherine was right in front, charging down the hill toward the corn field. Chris exploded down the grassy slope. A few more steps and she'd be in the field. Chris reached out. Her hair brushed his fingertips.

She hit a wall of corn stalks and vanished. Chris ducked and charged after her. The stalks slapped his face like whips. *Where is she?* He ran harder.

His lungs burned. He stopped and panted. *Wow. How far in am I?*

The corn stood three feet above his head and draped into a canopy, blocking the sun. There was no noise, as though the corn had sucked it out of the air, and now the corn felt menacing, as though it had thoughts, meaning, and purpose. He spun around. Someone was watching. A leaf rustled and it sounded as loud as a truck horn. He jumped and spun again. *Nothing.*

"Katherine?" His voice was swallowed by the vacuum of silence. "Katherine?"

The hair on the back of his neck stood up and he could hear his heart beating against his chest. He felt foolish.

"Katherine!"

Katherine growled from behind him.

"Wha…?"

Her hair flew over his head and whipped tears into his eyes. Katherine slammed onto his back, pulled her arms around his throat, and wrapped her legs around his waist. He stumbled, weaved left, then right, and fell forward onto a corn stalk with her piggy-backed on top of him. His face hit the ground, driving a cloud of dust into his throat. He choked and gagged.

Katherine giggled, kissed him on the cheek, and vanished. "Betcha can't catch me!"

Chris, stunned by the kiss, stared at the ground for a few seconds, jumped to his feet, and ran after her.

Chris hiked up the hill to the barn, matching his steps with Katherine's. Michael and Thomas were behind them. The sun had dropped behind the mountains. The cornfield looked dark, and the corn stalks shuffled like there were creatures scurrying through them. He was tired, but content after an afternoon of playing tag, talking, and lounging in the sun.

Swinging his arm wider, he brushed the backside of her hand with his. She turned her hand and opened it. He grasped it and squeezed. They glanced at each other and smiled. Chris imagined he'd feel like this if about to step off a tall building wearing a parachute. Was he excited or scared?

"7:00 AM?" Katherine asked as they approached the barn.

"Sure," Chris said, "we'll be up."

"We'll bring the horses. Oh, and have another bath."

Chris rolled his eyes and she frowned at him.

CHAPTER 16

Chris bolted. He was standing straight up in his sleeping bag.

How?

Squinting against a blinding light, he stepped and tumbled onto Michael.

Light?

A beam drove through the window and lit up the barn brighter than the midday sun. He threw up his arm. "Whah?"

The whup-whup sound of helicopter blades blew through the cracks. The walls breathed in and out like a wobble board, and dust rained from the rafters.

"Helicopter! Michael!"

"What the heck?" Michael asked.

"Helicopter! They found us. Come on!"

Chris jumped down the ladder. "Hurry up!" he yelled while running to the door.

Michael yelled, "Where are you going?"

Chris pushed open the door to a tornado of leaves and dust. The door slammed back in his face. He pushed hard and fell onto the ground. He closed his eyes and stumbled along the barn toward the river. The ground shook under his feet, and it struck him that this wasn't a dream.

Did Michael yell?

The beam of light swung over the roof and illuminated the ground beside him. He leapt forward and rolled under the trees as the helicopter moved to his side of the barn.

"Damn, Michael! Where are you?"

What am I doing out here anyway?

The searchlight combed the ground, fluttered along the barn wall, and paused on the door. The helicopter rose and disappeared behind the roof.

"Whew."

Chris pulled his legs under him, crouched in a sprint position, and realized he was running around in his underwear. The leaves lit up around him, and the helicopter appeared right above his head. He crawled under a bush and watched the searchlight wander over the trees to the boat. It glowed like a bowl of butterscotch ice cream.

"We're dead," Chris said. He ran back to the barn door, opened it, and rolled inside, hitting something soft.

"Ooof! Look out," Michael said.

Chris stood. "Did they see you?"

"No. I wasn't running around like a naked idiot. Did they see you?"

"Don't think so, but they saw the boat."

"Crap! What...what now?"

"Shush," Chris said, "can you hear it?"

"No," Michael said, "they're gone."

Chris felt dead tired. His eyes started to close. "I'm going back to bed."

"Yeah, but, shouldn't we run for it?"

Chris crawled up the ladder and into his sleeping bag, and dropped into black.

CHAPTER 17

The alarm clock screeched like a barn owl. Chris popped open his eyes as the clock jumped from a hay bale and cracked into his head. He grabbed it and hurled it at the wall.

"What? You're an idiot! That was Katherine's," Michael said.

Chris tried to focus on Michael but his eyes were blurry, and his tongue felt fuzzy and loose. "Do what?" He dropped his face into the hay.

Pain jolted through his head. "Ouch!" He grabbed the piece of straw jammed into his nose and threw it at Michael, who burst into laughter.

"Yuck, it's got a booger on it, and blood," Michael said.

"You deserved it, booger face."

"No need to get personal, Chris."

Chris peeled off his sleeping bag. "Let's go." He jumped up and looked around. "Where're my shoes?"

"Right beside you, ya goof. A little grumpy this morning?"

Chris flopped down and fought with his shoelaces. "To hell with it," he muttered. He left them untied.

They rolled up their sleeping bags and pushed them into the backpacks. Chris carried his pack down, threw it onto the ground, and stripped the wrapper off a granola bar. He nibbled it a grain at a time. The chilled, dark air intensified his unease, and he felt sick.

"Did you hear horses, Chris?"

Chris stopped chewing.

"Uh, yeah, I think so."

Michael dashed out. Chris sauntered after him. Katherine and Thomas led four horses toward them.

Chris' gut hurt.

"Grandpa wants us back by five o'clock," Katherine said. "This gives us ten hours, or four hours in one direction and a one hour break. We have about twenty miles to go, so we should be able to make it. We'll keep the horses at a trot for the most part, with walking and the odd canter."

"What's a canter?" Michael asked.

"Like a gallop, but slower," Thomas said.

"Oh."

Michael stroked a horse's neck. It neighed, shook its mane, and stomped its hoof on the ground by Michael's foot. He jumped back and yelped. "It's big. What if it throws me off?"

Chris detected a waver in Michael's voice.

"You'll die?" Thomas asked.

"Thomas!" Katherine grinned. "You wish. Don't worry, Michael. He won't. I'll show you. Hold the reins loosely. A gentle tug to stop. Pull the right rein over the horse's neck to turn left and the left rein over the horse's neck to turn right. A light kick with your heels to speed up.

"Can you help me with your pack, Chris?" Katherine asked.

"Sure."

"Pick it up and place it behind my saddle. I'll strap it down."

"Why your horse?" Chris asked.

"They're not going to like this. I'd rather Thomas and I dealt with it," she said.

"Okay, Chris, you're first," Katherine said while pulling up a horse. "Put your left foot into the stirrup, grab the horn on the saddle, and pull yourself up."

"No problem," Chris said, looking up to his horse. It was jet black with a white diamond on its forehead.

"What's the metal bar in its mouth?" Chris asked.

"Called a bit," Katherine said.

"Doesn't it hurt?"

"No, don't worry. Just don't pull the reins too hard."

Chris gazed into the horse's eye. "Is he laughing at me?"

Katherine glanced at the horse. "Probably."

I'm history, Chris thought. "What's his name?"

"Buck," Katherine said.

"Yeah, for buck-off," Thomas said. He giggled.

Chris glared at Thomas, lifted his foot past his waist, and placed it into the stirrup. He reached until his underarms stretched, and grabbed the saddle horn. He pulled with his hands and pushed his foot. The saddle shifted. He jumped off.

"Go ahead," Thomas said. "It won't fall."

Chris set his foot into the stirrup. "Here goes," he whispered. He pulled hard on the saddle horn and pushed his foot into the stirrup. He soared, came down, and smacked the saddle. His foot popped out of the stirrup. His right leg slipped under the horse. He flew over the other side and hit the ground.

"Oouff!" Pain bolted through his shoulder like someone drove a nail through it.

Michael and Thomas started to giggle.

Chris staggered up and brushed the dirt off his pants. His face grew hot and prickly. Great; another chance for Michael to make fun of him. He'd rather walk than get onto a stupid horse. He glanced at Katherine and she grinned at him, a warm and supportive grin. "Are you all right?"

Buck farted.

Thomas squealed.

Michael fell to his knees and lost control, laughing until his face turned red. He gasped for air.

"Here, let me help you," Katherine said. She grabbed Chris' foot and held it into the stirrup. Chris pulled himself into the saddle.

"Hold on, Michael," Thomas said. "I have a stool. I'm too short to reach the stirrup."

Thomas placed a stool by Michael's horse, and Michael stepped on it, put his foot in the stirrup and mounted his horse, making it look easy. He looked at Chris and beamed. Chris glared back.

Michael's horse was chocolate brown with a shiny, black mane. "What's his name?" Michael asked.

"Einstein," Thomas replied.

"Great. We'll have lots to talk about then."

Katherine and Thomas hopped onto their horses.

"Follow me," Katherine said. She gave her horse a soft kick with her heels. It broke into a trot. Thomas' horse moved in behind her. Buck surged ahead. Chris heard Einstein trotting behind him.

It felt like sitting on a jack hammer. Chris popped up and hit the saddle as Buck came up again, canning himself on each stride. He gripped the saddle horn and locked his knees to Buck's sides. They had moved only sixty feet. His knees were tired and his groin fired lightning bolts. Chris looked back. Michael clutched the saddle horn with both hands. His eyes were closed and his teeth clenched.

They cleared the barn and surrounding trees.

"Oh," Katherine said and stopped. Chris drew up beside her.

The cornfield lay beneath them, spreading north and west. It seemed to reach the mountains. The wind swayed the golden tassels and green leaves, like a human wave washing through the stands at a football game. The rising sun blanketed the field in a brilliant red aura. They gazed at the kaleidoscope of moving color, unable to continue.

"Beautiful," Katherine whispered.

"Yeah," Chris said, "as beautiful as you."

Katherine blushed. "Thank you, Chris. Let's go."

They trotted down the grass embankment to a dirt road running alongside the corn field. A dust devil swirled down the middle of it.

Chris bolted upright.

"Michael?" Chris said, "did you dream about a helicopter?"

"Last night? Yeah, sure felt real. I just about peed my...the same dream?"

Michael stared at Chris. "How?"

Katherine drew her horse up. "Whatsup?"

"No," Chris said, "You can't take us, a helicopter. It flew over the barn last night. They saw the boat."

"Better get moving then," Katherine said.

"No!" Chris yelled. "You can't get involved."

"Did you guys leave anything behind?" Katherine asked.

"Nope. We made sure."

"Either way, we have no idea your boat is there, right? Thomas and I just went on a ride."

"But."

"Enough, Chris. We're wasting time. We're going to canter. Hold on tight. Let's run four across so Thomas and I can keep an eye on you."

Katherine and Thomas broke into a gallop. Buck surged after them. Chris' legs flew up past his head, and his back walloped Buck's croup. He grabbed the reins and pulled. Buck reared up. Chris stood in his stirrups and threw his arms around Buck's neck. Buck came down with a jolt and lunged into a full gallop, throwing Chris' face into his mane. The ground whooshed by, and Chris felt dizzy and sick. He squeezed his knees and gripped tighter.

"Nine point eight outta ten," Michael yelled from behind.

Katherine slowed her horse a bit, bringing Michael and Chris up beside her. "This is a canter," she yelled. She laughed. "Come on, guys, sit up! Get your arms off his neck, Chris, and grab the reins."

Though his leg muscles burned, Chris felt better. The canter felt natural; balancing was hard, but the rhythm easier to follow, and the morning air cooled his face. Katherine's hair flowed behind her. Michael's jaw was set hard. He seemed to be in pain. Thomas hadn't stopped grinning since they started the canter about thirty minutes ago.

Katherine reined her horse to a trot. Buck followed suit. Chris' bum hit the saddle. He yelped with pain.

"Guys!" Katherine shouted. "Raise your bums on every second beat. Rise on the first and sit on the second. Watch me."

Chris copied Katherine's rhythm. His legs had to hold him up between trots, which made his muscles burn even more, but he wasn't getting canned.

Michael groaned, out of relief, Chris assumed.

Katherine brought her horse to a walk.

"We'll take the horses to the river for a drink. As you can see, the road ends here. We'll continue up the hill till we reach the mountains. It's gonna get steep."

Michael shifted in his saddle. "Great! We can get off."

"Don't," Thomas said. "You'll hurt so bad you won't wanna get back on."

"Wonderful," Chris grumbled.

Buck sloshed into the river up to his knees and dropped his mouth to the water. Chris leaned forward and stroked his neck.

"Is that a bird?" Michael asked.

Chris looked into the eastern sky. A black dot hovered in the horizon. "Don't know, Michael. It could be a bird, or a helicopter at a distance. What do you think, Katherine?"

Katherine stared and frowned. "I think we better get going," she said.

They rode single file up to an eternal field of yellow grass tall enough to brush the horses' bellies.

Michael swooned. His eyes were half closed and his teeth clenched.

"Michael, are you all right?" Chris asked.

"Yep. Doing great," Michael said.

Three hours had passed. The terrain was steep, the grass shorter, and coniferous trees surrounded them, filling the ninety-degree air with the odor of pine. The river barreled through a narrow valley more than ninety feet below. It ran east, coming from the mountains and emptying into the Keetchum.

"Another hour and we'll meet the river," Katherine yelled. "We'll stop there for lunch and rest the horses. Chris, Michael, you can continue from there."

Buck tripped on a rock and stumbled. Chris clutched his mane and gasped. The path dropped at a treacherous angle and Buck's rear was higher than his head, pushing Chris into the saddle horn. A step to his left, a vertical cliff cut the mountain in two and fell to the river below. The saddle swayed side to side, and Chris was sure it would slip off, throwing him down the cliff into the rapids. Katherine said they would reach the river in one hour about an hour ago, and Chris couldn't wait. His legs were on fire and his knees hurt like they'd been smashed with boulders.

They reached the bottom of the hill and plunged into a dense coniferous forest. The air cooled. Tree stumps created black humps in the ground, like trolls hobbling together, preparing to attack. Chris looked back at Michael. Michael stared into the forest and his eyes were wide, his irises sparkling. Chris wondered if he was crying.

Chris couldn't see the river, but could hear it, an ominous sound as though a thousand people were crashing cymbals together. He pictured trolls, long yellow teeth grinning as they crashed their cymbals. He smirked.

The trail flattened and turned to the right. They rounded the curve and broke into a grassy clearing. The river, crystal clear and overlaid with eddies and whirlpools, gurgled alongside the clearing.

Katherine stopped her horse, hopped off, and led it to the river.

Thomas popped onto the ground and followed.

"Whoa, boy," Chris said. He swung his right leg back over Buck and dropped it, but couldn't find the ground. He squeaked and stretched his leg farther. His muscles were taught and felt like they would snap. His toe touched as Buck started to walk, forcing him to hop on one foot. "Help!" He tripped and fell and dangled from the stirrup, scaring Buck into a trot. His head bounced over a rock and his T-shirt tore off. Roots, branches, and gravel dug stinging scratches into his back.

"Whoa, Buck!" Thomas appeared and grabbed the reins. "Easy, boy." He eased Buck to a halt, grabbed Chris' foot, and pulled it from the stirrup.

Michael laughed. "That's the funniest thing I've ever seen!"

"Actually, that was a dangerous spot," Thomas sad. "Chris was lucky he didn't get hurt."

Chris rolled onto his stomach. "Fine then!" he yelled at Michael. "You try it, Einstein!"

Michael swung his right leg over and leaned his stomach onto the saddle just like Thomas had. He pulled his foot out of the stirrup and hopped to the ground like a pro.

"Jerk," Chris whispered.

"Hah!" Michael said.

Michael stepped forward and collapsed onto his face. A plume of dust blew up around him.

Chris, Thomas, and Katherine screamed with laughter.

Michael turned red. He looked crazy. He opened his mouth, said nothing, and closed it, then grinned.

Katherine and Thomas removed the packs and tossed them onto the ground.

Chris' bum burned like hot coals. He pulled his leg under him and pushed his foot down. He wobbled and fell over.

Michael crawled like a baby.

I'm such an idiot, Chris thought. Katherine must think this is hilarious.

"I bet I can walk before you can," Michael yelled.

Chris pushed his bum into the air and bear walked twenty steps. Pine cones cut his hands. He dropped onto his knees and lowered his bum to his feet.

"Ow, ow, ow." He popped up, straightened his knees, and

stepped as though strapped into braces. "No wonder cowboys walk like this," he said. He looked at Michael, who still crawled through the grass. "Hah! Beat ya!"

Chris staggered to a black rock the size of a car. Katherine and Thomas were sitting on it, eating sandwiches. Chris crawled up beside Katherine and watched Michael swagger toward them. He crawled onto the rock and lay on his back.

Chris looked up. Fluffy clouds drifted overhead. He pondered the rock's origins. Did a glacier grind it smooth and deposit it? Did aliens transport it?

Michael started snoring. Chris smiled. He knew that sleep was the only way out of this nightmare. At least Michael was, for a few minutes, at peace.

Chris looked at Katherine. "I'm going to miss you," he said.

"Me, too," she replied. "We'll see each other when you get back home. Right?"

"You bet." Chris felt giddy, out of control. His heart pounded.

He leaned over and pressed his lips to hers.

Her body stiffened. She placed her hands against his chest and pushed back, filling him with regret.

Screwed up again, Chris.

She softened and pressed into him. Her hands crept around his back. She closed her mouth, pulled away, and brushed her lips against his. Her lips felt like marshmallows. She looked into his eyes, smiled, and drew in, parting her mouth. He touched his lips to hers, allowing her to guide him.

"That's just not right!" Thomas bellowed.

Chris jumped back.

Michael bolted. "Are we leaving?"

"I sure hope so!" Thomas said.

Chris felt his face turn scarlet. His heart beat wildly. He looked into the ground, both elated and embarrassed.

They threw on their packs.

"Thanks for everything," Michael said to Thomas. He shook Thomas' hand.

"Uh-huh," Thomas replied.

Michael shook Katherine's hand.

Chris shook Thomas' hand.

Chris hugged Katherine.

"Thanks," Chris said. "Can't wait to see you again."

"You be careful!" Katherine said. "We'll keep an eye on the news. Call us if you have to."

"Will do, and you be careful, too."

Chris turned to the mountains and looked up. "Holy! They're big.

Katherine and Thomas trotted past the barn. It was five o'clock and the trip was uneventful. The smell of apple pie made Katherine's mouth water.

She looked to Thomas. "Hurry up. Can't have pie till we groom the horses!"

They broke into a trot and rounded the corner. Grandma and Grandpa's house was sided in yellow wood slats and had an old fashioned porch around the front of it. A second barn was located about one hundred and fifty feet in front of it. "Wow! A Hummer!" Katherine exclaimed. "What's that doing out here?"

CHAPTER 18

Chris stumbled over a fractured rock, threw his arms out, and dropped onto his right thumb, bending it to his wrist. A dust cloud broke from the ground and exploded into his eyes.

"Ahhhgggg," he screamed and shook his head, spraying a ribbon of sweat into the air. He rubbed his eyes, forcing dirt and salt into them. They stung. He pushed his forearms into the ground, pulled his legs under him, and staggered up. The backpack, like a block of lead, constricted the blood flow to his hands. He watched his thumb balloon and turn purple. He raised it to shield his face from the low-lying sun and surveyed their surroundings.

They stood on a ridge inside a valley more than four football fields laid end to end in width. Granite peaks towered nine-thousand feet, enclosing the north and south sides of the valley as far as he could see.

A thick carpet of Subalpine Fir trees, sixty feet in height, claimed the valley floor. They became stunted and twisted as they crawled up the steep mountain slopes, losing their fight against the barren soil, deep snow, and unrelenting wind.

The trees had skinny trunks not more than ten inches in diameter and swayed, groaned, and clapped together, brought to life by the howling wind from the west. It was eerie. Chris half expected a tsunami to burst through the head of the valley, sweeping up rocks, trees, and animals in its wake. He felt small.

He pulled the comforting odor of pine deep into his lungs and lifted his T-shirt, allowing the cool mountain air to dry the sweat off his stomach.

He stepped forward and stumbled again. "How 'bout we spend the night?" he called.

"Love to," Michael said from behind.

Chris heard him stumble and gasp.

Chris slid the pack off his aching shoulders, unbuckled the waist strap, and dropped it to the ground, flattening a patch of ivory colored flowers. He flopped onto the pack. Pain throbbed from his feet with a rhythmic boom, coursed through his legs, into his head, and pounded his ears like kettledrums. The thumping pulled the distant rush of water, swish of the wind blown trees, and buzzing of dragonflies into a full blown symphony. Strauss, Blue Danube, he thought as Michael hit the ground beside him.

They stared at the cirrus clouds laying flat against the sky, mesmerized.

"Hey, Chris, that one looks like Katherine."

Chris' stomach twisted with a heart-wrenching pang. "Shut up, Michael." He shivered. "Better set up camp. It'll be dark soon."

Chris yanked the tent out of his pack and walked to a small opening between the trees. He threw it down and spread it out. Michael assembled the shock cords. They inserted them into the tent and popped it into shape. Orange nylon panels held into a peaked dome with the cords, created a space tall enough for them to sit in. They tossed thin grey pads onto the floor and threw the sleeping bags on top.

"It looks lonely," Michael said.

"Yep. Wait till dark. We'll feel like the last two people on earth. Let's go. We need water."

Michael grabbed two water bottles from his pack, clear hard plastic, one cherry red and the other yellow. Chris pulled a blue bottle and the water filter from his pack. They plunged into the dark forest to the south. The sweat soaking Chris' t-shirt turned chilly. He surveyed the fallen trees littering the forest floor and groaned. He plodded to the first one and swung his leg over. Dead branches snagged his jeans and snapped like peanut brittle. His foot touched the ground just as his groin came to rest on the trunk. He grinned. Michael was a full foot shorter than he was.

Using the river's gurgling as a guide, he estimated it to be half-a-mile away. "It's gonna be a tough hike, Michael."

Chris panted. His jeans were torn and his arms scratched. He looked back at Michael, whose face was contorted into a permanent sneer. A half hour had passed since they left the tent.

A huge patch of Canada Buffalo Berry, almost six feet in height, guarded the river. Chris pushed the twisted branches aside and dove in. Berries popped under his feet, spreading slippery fluid onto the ground and staining his runners blood red. The fuzzy leaves were covered in spider webs and sticky stuff that smeared onto his hands, clothes, and face.

"Agghh," Michael yelled.

"What?"

"Spiders, I hate them!"

"How did you get that tarantula into my slipper?"

"When driven, I'll do about anything."

"Do you smell that, Michael?"

"Yeah, you should have used deodorant this morning."

"I...you...jeez, shut up! No, damp moss. The river's close by."

Chris pushed through and onto the river shore.

Green and red rocks, shaped like dinosaur eggs and polished by the fast moving water, broke the river's surface into foaming rapids and swirling eddies. Chris could almost jump to the other shore if he took a run at it. He flopped down, stripped off his shoes and socks, and placed his feet and swollen thumb into the ice cold water. He gasped.

"Try it, Michael. It's great."

"I was gonna to drink that, Chris."

Chris grinned. He grabbed the filter, screwed the blue water bottle into it, tossed the clear plastic tubing into the river, and pumped the lever. He followed the water up the tube and through the porcelain filter, leaving behind dirt, bacteria, and viruses before trickling into the bottle. The bottle filled within ten minutes, he guessed, but the throbbing in his hand felt like being hit by a hammer with every push against the lever.

"Here, Michael, the rest are yours."

Chris slid his hand into the river and watched Michael.

"What?" Chris asked.

Michael's eyes darted through the forest. He turned back and looked to the mountains. "Gettin' dark."

"Yeah, sun's disappeared. Finish up and we'll go."

They turned from the river and pushed through the bushes. Shadows blended into a singular darkness, with the odd stab of light breaking through the treetops and illuminating dead branches jumping out of fallen trees, grey like old people fingers. Stumps were caves, doorways leading from the depths of hell. The grass whispered and waved like flowing white hair. The trees groaned and shuddered in a language, Chris guessed, they could understand. Swallowing his uneasiness, he pushed on.

Chris glanced at his watch. Fluorescent markers glowed back. Fifteen minutes had passed.

"What's that sound, Michael?"

They stopped and listened.

"Oh no!" Michael groaned. "We went in a circle."

Chris dashed over a crest to the river. He looked behind him. He recognized nothing. He wanted to scream.

"We won't survive out here tonight."

A sound like the crack of a leather whip echoed through the trees. Dirt sprayed into Chris' face.

A black shadow rose over their heads. It drifted toward them without sound.

Michael whined. His fear electrified the air.

Shimmering eyes rose from the earth.

A gush of warm air blew back Chris' hair.

"Sme...smelling us," Chris said.

The thing snorted like a bomb blast.

"Look out!" Chris yelled.

It charged.

Chris jumped behind a tree. Michael froze.

"Move, Mike!" Chris screamed.

Michael threw a water bottle into its head. It cut left and thundered by. Michael collapsed. The bottle whumped into his chest.

"Are you all right?" Chris asked.

"S-s-s-s-Sasquatch?" Michael squealed.

Chris grabbed Michael's hand and pulled him up. "Sasquatch? No, a moose, I think. I never really thought of a sasquatch."

"Are, are you sure?"

"Did you see the rack? It was like five feet wide. I'm glad he cut left. Moose weigh over a thousand pounds; would've crushed you into Jello.

"Come on then, let's go." Chris said.

"How can you be so flippin' cheerful?" Michael asked. He croaked like a frog.

"One, we were charged by a moose and lived to tell about it. Two, I think I know how to find the trail."

Chris pushed through the forest, using the darkness of a mountain peak as a guide. He acted calm, but his body shook, and his legs felt like elastic bands.

"How the hell could you forget a first aid kit and flashlight? Damn lucky you didn't get us killed!" he whispered.

His runner crunched. *Gravel.*

He turned west, guessing they broke through before their camp. He could see nothing, but walked with long strides.

"Watch for the tent. We might walk right, oh, there it is."

Chris dropped down and crawled, waving his hands in front. His fingertips scratched nylon. He yanked the pack open, reached inside, pulled out a flashlight, and flicked it on. He swung the crisp light around their camp. The trees seemed closer. The light tried to stab through them, but was swallowed by the black trunks and branches.

Michael's eyes bulged like globe lights. He stared into the forest like he'd seen a ghost.

"What's the matter, Michael?" Chris asked.

Michael didn't move. "Nuh, nothing."

Chris grinned. "Knocks the smart-ass right outta ya, doesn't it?"

Michael turned and glared at him. "I'm hungry."

They threw on their sweaters and collected twigs and moss from the forest floor. Chris lit a fire. He sat back and watched Michael dump a box of KD into a pot of water.

They sat on a fallen tree and slurped the noodles.

Darkness pushed inwards, collapsing the fire into a tiny circle, barely strong enough to illuminate their faces.

Chris looked into the forest and shivered. "Better clean the dishes."

"Shoot!" Chris yelped. "We have to hang the backpacks!"

"How bout we put the food into a nylon bag and haul it up?"

"Good idea."

They stuffed food, pots, and pans into a tote bag. Michael tied a rope around it. Chris took the bag and stumbled thirty paces into the forest. He wrapped his arms around a tree and shimmied up it, holding the rope. The tree waved back and forth, as though trying to throw him off.

"Michael, flashlight!"

Michael swung the beam up toward him. Chris gripped the trunk with his left arm and fed the rope over a branch and down to Michael.

Michael pulled the bag up and tied the rope to a tree.

Chris slid down.

"Let's go."

They dashed back to the camp.

Chris tossed dirt onto the fire, collapsing the darkness onto them.

"We're at the top of the world," Michael whispered.

Chris looked up. The Milky Way lit the night sky like a full moon. "Yeahhhh."

"Look!" Chris cried. "The Big Dipper!"

"Yeah, hey! Do you see those stars to your left?"

"Which ones?"

"Over there." Michael pointed with the flashlight. "See, the triangle?"

"Uh, yeah. I think so."

"Look straight up from the top of the triangle. Two stars, one on top of the other. Go right of the top star and you'll find another one. From there come straight down, just below the triangle. There's another one. Continue down and to the right and you'll see a couple more, close to each other."

"What? It looks like nothing. At least the dipper looks like a pot!"

"It's Gemini, Chris."

"Gemini?"

"Yeahhh. Do you know the story of Gemini?" Michael's eyes twinkled. He seemed lost in another world.

"No," Chris said.

"Gemini is a story about twins, two brothers, Castor and Pollux. The brothers were so close that when Castor died his immortal brother begged Zeus to share his immortality with his brother. Zeus placed the brothers together in the sky. After he placed them in the sky, he put a bright star in each ones head. Those are the two bright stars above the triangle."

"Oh. Don't suppose you'd pay this Zeus guy a visit if I died?"

Chris asked.

"Might be pushing it, but, yeah, I'd consider it."

For a moment, Chris felt like he'd won a trophy. He grabbed the flashlight from Michael and pointed it in the sky. "Look! The Little Dipper!"

Michael's teeth flashed, revealing a smile. "Uh-huh."

"Stars aren't near this bright in town," Chris whispered. "Michael?"

"Yeah?"

"I did drink furniture polish once."

"Accident?"

"No."

Michael turned and looked at him. "What then?"

"When I was eight I went through the kitchen cupboard, under the sink. I pulled out all the bottles with a skull and cross bones, looking for the deadliest one."

"Why the heck would you do that?"

"I...I wanted her to notice me. I thought she would, if I got really sick."

"Mom?"

"Yeah."

"So, what happened?"

"She made me drink salt water till I puked, and put me to bed early."

"Didn't work, heh?"

"Not at all. My throat hurt real bad for awhile."

Michael punched Chris' shoulder. "Sorry, Chris."

"No prob. I got over it. Let's go to bed."

Chris walked to the tent, unzipped it, and crawled in.

"Come on. Early morning coming our way."

Michael crawled through and closed the zipper. They snuggled into their warm sleeping bags and fell asleep.

A falling star streaked through the sky overhead.

A black creature pawed at the ground alongside the river, digging up a cache of rotten fish.

CHAPTER 19

Michael flew through chilly air over a still lake. Black clouds forced him close to the water's surface. He sped toward an island, a rock. Or did it speed toward him? It sat low in the water. A light grey, it looked like a beacon against the darkness around it. A mound appeared on top. He couldn't quite see, but he knew. It was her. He flew faster and faster. Terror clawed his guts. He couldn't stop. He whimpered.

All was still.

Was he awake?

He held his hand in front of his face and saw nothing.

His tummy rumbled.

Pine branches tore at each other like Velcro. The tent billowed and collapsed. The creek gurgled in the distance. It was freezing, below zero, or close to it. He longed to stay inside the sleeping bag, but his stomach growled.

"Damn you," he whispered, flipping onto his side. He swept his hand over the ground. It bounced over roots, rocks, and branches set under the cold tent floor and hit the flashlight. He grabbed it and pressed the button. An intense beam of blue/white light struck the tent top.

Michael's legs started shaking. He furled his brow and concentrated, tightening his thighs and calves. They shook more. He relaxed. He'd let them shake. Maybe they would stop themselves.

He had to pee.

He lay down and pointed the flashlight at Chris. Chris' skin was shiny and tight, and a blue-grey color. He looked dead.

Michael cursed his feelings of doom. This quest wouldn't end well. The blue lady in his visions; she enforced it. He wanted to tell Chris, but no. Chris wouldn't believe him anyway. And what choice did they have, but to continue?

Michael hated the visions. He couldn't escape them, and they all became true. He'd been preparing for the home invasion since he was five. A vision drove him to build the hide-out and put cameras all over the house. And if the blue lady was who he thought she was. Michael shuddered.

His stomach growled. Reaching into his pocket, he pulled out a granola bar, removed the crinkly wrapper, and bit down. It shattered under his teeth.

"Yuck." It was old, and tasted like sawdust and sucked the moisture from his mouth. The hair on the back of his neck stood up. He stopped chewing and listened.

That smell. Dead fish?

The wind whistled.

An owl hoo'd overhead.

A branch cracked right beside the tent.

He jumped.

Stop it, Michael. It's your bloody imagination!

He rolled onto his back and stared into the tent top. It rose past his face and up to the peak in the centre. He crunched into the bar.

His heart pounded like a speed bag. Yeah, like that one in that Rocky movie, he thought.

Why?

Black claws tore through the tent.

"WHAT THE...?"

They razed down, shredding the nylon like candy wrapper. Pain streaked through Michael's nose. Warm blood rained onto his cheek.

I'm dreaming.

A black creature pounced over him and roared.

Yellow teeth clamped onto his head.

The stench of rotting flesh burst into his nose. Slobber streamed down his throat. He choked and spewed into the creature's mouth.

CHAPTER 20

The animal roar smashed Chris' sleep like a train wreck. He woke disoriented and panicked. He flopped over. Puke splattered his face. He wrenched the flashlight from Michael's fist and drove it into the creature's eye.

The creature reared and vanished.

Michael leapt to his knees and screamed. Chris froze with the flashlight held like a knife above his head.

Michael threw his arms around Chris' neck and wailed. "What was that Chris? What the heck was that?"

"Let, go, Michael." Chris wheezed and gagged at the stench. He pried his hands between them and pushed Michael away, then grabbed him and pulled him back tight.

"Ssshhhh, Michael, it's all right. It's gone now. It was a bear."

"Why us, Chris? Why is this happening to us? I want to go home! I want to go home!"

"It's all right. I've got you."

Chris swung the flashlight through the trees. He could feel the bear just outside the flashlight's reach, watching, pacing, planning.

"Are you all right, Michael? Are you hurt?"

"She's dead, Chris!"

"Who?"

"Mom! She's dead!"

"Sshush, no she isn't Michael. Don't worry. We'll get there. We'll save them."

Chris' teeth chattered. The cold air had assaulted them for the past hour.

The stars released their hold on night and surrendered it to the morning sun.

"Come on, Michael. Let's get out of here. It's 6:00 AM."

"But, it's gonna get me!"

"Michael! We've got no roof over our heads!"

Michael wailed. "That thing!"

Chris grabbed Michael and shouted in his face. "Get a hold of yourself. I'll start a fire. Pour some water into the pot. We'll heat some for oats and use the rest to clean up the puke."

Michael sloshed water out of the bottle onto the ground, his lap, and the small stainless steel pot. He placed the pot on Chris' fire. They sat and rocked, watching the lid, waiting for steam.

"What kind of oats, Chris?"

"Cinnamon roll."

"My favorite."

The wind had died. Light streamed through the valley from the east.

Chris poured some steaming water into two bowls of oats and squirted dish soap into the pot. Michael dipped a tea towel in and rubbed his face until it glowed red.

Michael looked at Chris and wrinkled his nose. "I can't get the stench out."

"Yeah, but at least the puke is gone, mostly."

Chris walked to the tent and picked up the torn half. "It's in one piece. I think we can repair it. Won't be waterproof, but it'll keep us warm."

They cleaned off Michael's sleeping bag and stuffed the packs.

"I'll take the rope," Michael said.

"No way, it's too heavy, and you've got the food."

"Shut up! I'm in no mood."

They bolted onto the trail.

"Hope we don't meet him again," Michael said.

"Could have been a her."

CHAPTER 21

Michael slipped on a chunk of shale and stumbled toward the cliff. His pack pulled him over the side. He teetered on the edge and screamed, wind-milled his arms, and fell to the ground just before toppling to his death..

"Slow down," Chris yelled from behind. "Are you all right?"

"Fine," Michael said.

"How 'bout some lunch?" Chris asked.

Michael didn't move. He threw his final scraps of energy to his lungs and panted. His back muscles crossed the threshold of extreme pain to an intense, throbbing numbness. He placed his hand against the cliff wall, pushed himself up, brushed off his pants, and peered ahead. Cut into a cliff, the trail wasn't much wider than he, and littered with loose shale. It ramped up at a grueling pitch, snaked around, and disappeared far ahead. He peeked down. The river raged sixty feet below. Contained by sheer cliffs it boiled and screamed through a narrow ravine. Michael's head spun. He pulled away and pressed into the rock wall behind him. What's it so angry about? he thought.

Hunger pangs tore through his stomach.

"Let's find shade," he said.

A dwarfed evergreen tree, curled and twisted like a dragon, gripped a crevice cut into the cliff side, blocking the path. Michael grabbed it, sucked in a breath, and pushed over the cliff.

His foot slipped and kicked out a piece of shale. It fell, shattered into the cliff, and vanished into the rapids without a sound.

"Katherine told me that people ride horses on this trail. Could you imagine?" Chris asked.

Michael pulled himself around to the other side. "No flippin' way."

"Watch that one, Chris," he called.

"Almost there Mi..."

Michael stopped. *Weird.*

He turned around.

"How the hell do you vanish into thin air?" Michael yelled. He swallowed.

"CHRIS! WHERE ARE YOU?"

"Are you, are you..." The canyon echoed back.

The tree shuddered against a wind gust. The rapids grew louder. Michael's skin prickled. He rubbed his arms and scuttled back, flopping onto his stomach and peering over the ledge.

"No!"

Chris lay face-down nine feet below on a shelf cut into the cliff. His left leg bobbed over the edge, pulling him down.

Michael threw his pack off and grabbed the buckle securing the rope. He fumbled with it, but it wouldn't loosen. He tore it off. He tied both ends of the rope to the tree. "Hope this little guy can hold us," he mumbled.

He threw the rope over alongside Chris, creating two climbing ropes. He grabbed one, pulled up fifteen feet of it, and tied it around his waist. He pulled up the slack, leaned back, and rappelled down. The tree flopped over. A root ripped with a gut wrenching pop. Michael ignored it and dropped to Chris.

He sat in front of Chris' head and pushed into the cliff wall. He pulled Chris' leg up and crossed it over the right one. He grabbed the other rope, pushed it under Chris' waist, tied a loop around it, and fashioned another loop around Chris' crotch.

He leaned back and panted.

Chris, unconscious, would flop like a rag doll if he fell. The rope would most likely slide through his arms. The loop through his crotch would stop that but Michael was concerned it would flip him over, head down, and he'd slip out anyway.

"Oh well, best I can do," he said.

Michael looked at Chris' pack. If Chris fell, the pack would add another forty pounds of dead weight. He doubted he could pull Chris up anyway, but this would worsen his chances.

"Oh, the laptop."

Michael frowned. If Chris fell into the river with his pack the laptop would be lost. Michael couldn't complete the mission without it.

He pulled up some of his rope and tied it to Chris' pack. He pushed his hand under Chris' waist, unbuckled his pack, and pulled his arms out of the shoulder straps.

He looked up to the tree. If Chris fell, the tree would probably tear out anyway. Then, they'd both be done for.

He placed his hand in front of Chris' nose and felt a puff of air. There was no sign of blood. Michael felt behind Chris' head. He had a large lump on the back of it. Most of his stitches from the bathroom fall were scraped off. *One way to remove them, I guess.*

Water roared through the dark chasm below. The sun burned his scalp. How long had Chris been out? Five minutes? What if he didn't wake up? What if he stopped breathing?

A loud thump vibrated the ground from above.

Avalanche?

The ground shook. Rocks rained down. Michael threw himself over Chris' head.

Another thump, a piece of shale shattered into his back.

"Ouch!"

Michael lifted his arm against the falling debris and looked up. "Oh!"

The grizzly bear growled. It reared onto its hind legs, stood ten feet high, and crashed its front paws into the ground with a massive thump.

"Get outta here, puke face! I've had enough of your attitude!"

The bear waved its head from side to side, grunted, and disappeared.

Whew. That was easy, Michael thought.

Michael heard sounds from above. Tearing? Chewing?

"What the heck?" he muttered.

Rustling?

Cloth. Nylon?

"No!"

The tent floated by. Michael lunged out to catch it but missed. He slipped and fell. The rope snapped taut. He bobbed up and down like a fish on the end of a line. He heard a root pop. He leapt onto the shelf in one bound. The tent collapsed, fell to the river, and vanished.

Michael heard crunching; Granola bars and potato chips. *I wonder if he's taking the wrap off.*

A full box of KD bounced off of Chris' head and fell into the river below.

"It tastes better before I throw it up, you jerk!" Michael screamed.

Chris lifted his head, winced at the sun, and peered at Michael. "Ouch! Where am I?"

"You're just in time for dinner."

An empty salmon can landed on Chris' back.

"Whah?" Chris asked.

"You fell off the path. I've got you tied up. Don't look down and don't move. Oh, and our friendly night stalker is eating our food."

"The bear?"

"Yep."

Chris groaned and laid his head back down.

All went silent.

"Do you think it's gone?" Michael asked.

"Dunno, only one way to find out, though," Chris said while pulling himself into a sitting position. He grimaced. "Man, I can't believe how much this hurts!"

"Not as much as a getting beaten by a hoe, I'm sure."

"It'll be harder getting up than down," Chris said.

Michael grinned. "Less for me. Getting down was easy for you."

Chris grimaced. "You're such a jerk! Do you ever stop?"

"No."

Chris looked up to the trail. "I'll go first. You've got my pack tied to you."

Chris gripped the rope, placed his feet on the cliff, and pulled. He stepped up with his right foot and pivoted. Swinging sideways, his shoulder crashed into the cliff. He fell onto the ledge.

"Spread your legs wider apart," Michael suggested.

Chris tied a knot into the rope as high as he could reach. He tied another at his chest.

"Should be able to hold on to these."

Chris grabbed a knot, placed his foot onto a toe hold, and pushed and pulled himself up.

"Ahhhhhh. It's cutting into my sore hand."

"Keep going, Chris. You can do it."

Chris jumped to the last knot and placed his left foot higher. One more step and his head would be level with the path.

"Go, Chris, Go! You can do it!" Michael yelled.

Chris swung his arm over the trail, pushed his feet into the cliff, and vanished.

"Chris?"

"Doesn't look good up here, Michael. He chewed through your backpack and ate everything."

"Great," Michael mumbled. "I'm starving."

Michael watched Chris' pack inch by him, past his head, and up to the path where it disappeared.

"Your turn, Michael."

Michael grabbed the rope and, with Chris pulling, scuttled up the cliff wall. He pulled himself onto the trail and lay on his back.

"Here, drink this." Chris passed him a water bottle. "Let's get out of here."

"What if we meet the bear?"

"No worries. I can run faster than you."

"Thanks."

"Pleasure's all mine." Chris smiled.

CHAPTER 22

Chris pummeled his toes into the path, blowing dust plumes past his knees. Shadows were long and the air cool. Poplar and birch trees surrounded them, leaving only a thin strip of sky. His t-shirt was drenched with sweat. He sucked dust through his parched mouth and into his lungs. He coughed.

"One small step for mankind," he mumbled. "How much farther can we go without food and water?"

He stopped and waited for Michael to catch up.

"I bet the lake is over that crest," Chris said, pointing ahead.

"I hope so."

Chris trudged on. The crest was about five hundred steps up.

He crossed his fingers as they breached the top.

"Whah-hooo!"

He looked into a bowl of emerald green water surrounded with towering snow-capped peaks and blue spruce trees. A long path of boulders, the remains of a rock slide, swept down the southern peak and into the lake.

Chris heard a faint noise, like a toilet flushing. "What's that?"

"Dunno."

They watched. A loud pop and a sound like a rack of snooker balls breaking rang through the valley.

"Can't see it Michael."

Chris saw some movement on the rock slide and heard another pop. Michael pointed to a boulder the size of a Volkswagen Beetle, barreling down the rock slide. It hopped into the air and cracked the lake surface with a whump.

"I hope that's normal," Michael said.

"Yeah. Me, too. You think this is an extinct volcano?"

"Looks like it, perfectly round. Hope it stays dormant tonight."

A steady wind blew into their faces, shaking the trees, pushing glacier cooled air through their clothes and forcing waves onto the lakeshore. Chris shivered.

"Better get our sweaters on," Chris said.

They threw their packs onto the ground.

"Thomas," Michael said.

Chris looked at him. "Huh?"

"What would we have done without him?"

"Whadya mean?"

"Sweaters and a rope. He saved our butts more than once today."

"Heh. Give him a hug when we get back. You'll scare the bejeezers out of him."

Michael laughed, jumped up, and plunged down the rocky trail. Chris grabbed his pack and tore after him.

"Beat ya!" Chris yelled. He dropped his pack and ran to the water.

Bull trout swam under the water line.

"Looks delicious, Chris."

"Yep, all we need is a fishing rod and some butter to fry them in. They're so close I can almost touch them."

"Sushi?" Michael asked.

"You catch 'em. I'll cut 'em."

Chris' stomach rumbled

They shivered as a silent breeze brushed by.

"It's cold, and we don't have a tent," Chris said.

"Maybe we should walk to the other shore. We'll be sheltered from the wind there," Michael said.

"I wanted to hear it from you. It's closer to the avalanche, but I'm willing to risk it. Let's go."

A boulder cracked off the cliff with a loud bang and plunged into the lake.

Chris groaned and slung his pack on. The shore was covered in oblong rocks about the size of cantaloupes. He balanced on one. It wobbled. He slipped and fell onto his elbow. "Ouch; careful, Michael. Hey look, a moose."

"Great."

The moose waded through the waters by the mouth of the river on the west end.

"Do you think that's the same one?" Michael asked.

"Uh, I think it's smaller."

"Remember yesterday? Better hurry before we lose daylight," Chris said.

"Don't wanna remember yesterday."

Michael pulled the hatchet from Chris' pack. "Need to make a shelter."

Chris turned toward the forest. "Follow me." He stepped into the moss, so spongy and deep it swallowed his foot. He pushed forward, past a bolder and a long cliff wall. He stopped and smiled. A fallen tree lay north to south in front of him, creating a natural wind break on its east side about as high as Chris' waist. "We need some small trees, Michael, about as thick as your leg. We're going to make a lean-to."

Chris looked to his left and spotted one. Without bark, it was grey with death. He yanked it up and passed it to Michael. "Hack off the branches. We need about twelve more of them."

They lay the trees, one end on the ground and the other on top of the fallen log, creating a lean-to. Chris staggered through the forest cutting pine branches while Michael gathered them. They covered the lean-to with the branches and tossed a bunch inside, creating a soft, raised bed in case it rained. They heaved up a fallen tree and placed it over the north side of the lean-to. Chris placed the packs over the south side.

"Doors."

They stepped back and admired their house.

"Good job, Michael! Let's start a fire and pretend to eat. In fact, why don't you start the fire tonight? I'll gather wood."

"Sure. Jeez, I'm hungry."

"Think about it, no food, no bear."

"Ha. I'm sure he'll find you tasty."

Michael dug out a circle of moss until he reached dirt. He encircled the hole with rocks and added crumpled newspaper into the middle of them. He tossed on some tree lichen, grass, pine cones, and dead branches, and lit the newspaper. The flames caught the pine branches and roared up past their waists.

They pulled up a fallen tree and sat down on it.

Chris stared into the coals. Their orange glow ebbed in the gusting breeze.

"How are we going to get to that island?" Chris asked.

"No idea. We're not gonna swim it."

Chris looked at the lake. It was black and dead calm. "We need a boat. I think we'll figure it out when we get there. Nine days, I hope Mom and Dad are all right."

"I wonder if they got into some kind of trouble at the lab?" Michael asked.

Chris grabbed a stick and stirred the coals. "Did you ever check the lab out?"

"Are you kidding? I couldn't let the place go. I spent weeks trying to find out what went on in there."

"What did you find?"

"Basically, nothin'. They design military stuff."

Chris stopped stirring. "Weapons?"

"What else would you design for the military?"

Chris grinned. "Food rations, socks? I asked dad and mom, but they'd never talk about it. Hey, didn't they seem a little spaced out over the past few months?"

Michael spat into the fire. "When did I ever see them?"

"Good point. Hey! Did I tell you about the e-mail?"

"What e-mail?"

"Between Dad and Greg. On their computer. Dad was talking about a machine of some kind and a fruit fly."

"Fruit fly? Serious?"

"Yeah, he was excited about it. He made the fly disappear or something. Greg said he'd get a turbine for power."

"Great. Now Dad's a magician. Fruit fly? I didn't know Greg worked at the lab."

Chris poked at the coals. "Me neither. How 'bout Jane? Maybe she's in on it, too."

"Maybe her brother owns the lab?"

"Could be, you don't think Jane and Greg are behind this, do you?"

Chris saw a shadow move in the forest. He stared at it.

"You think Jane and Greg would want to hurt us?" Michael said.

Chris looked into the fuzzy sky.

"I can't believe that, Michael." A tear escaped from his eye. He looked down and wiped it off his cheek. "I can't believe that."

Another boulder hit the lake with a whump.

"I wish those rocks would stop. It's weird." Chris said.

Chris checked his watch, 11:00 PM. Chilled air invaded the circle of warmth cast by the fire. Michael sighed, grabbed a bottle of water, and poured it onto the coals. They hissed, spat, and lost, plunging the campground into darkness. Chris looked up. He couldn't see a single star.

They crawled into the shelter. Chris propped the backpacks beside him, wiggled into his sleeping bag, and rolled onto his back. He could sense the lean-to above him, but couldn't see it.

"Michael?"

No answer. Chris closed his eyes. He remembered his first night camping. He thought a giant would step on his tent and squash him. This was worse. He shivered.

The moose stumbled beside their shelter. It sniffed, pawed the ground, and snorted.

Another boulder broke loose and tumbled down. Like dominos, several cascaded along with it. They hit the water with a boom. The moose bolted.

CHAPTER 23

A loon call echoed over the lake.

"Chris?"

"Yeah, a loon, eerie, isn't it?"

"What time is it?" Michael asked.

The loon called again.

"Just a sec. I can't see a thing."

Chris stared into his luminescent watch until the green glow of the hands came into focus. "5:00"

A second loon started a canon, erupting into a barrage of noise so loud Chris didn't hear the remainder of his sentence. Echoes proliferated the pair of loons into six, ten, fifteen. Their calls skimmed the lake, struck the rockslide and glacier, swirled through the trees, and dove into Chris' heart. Their song was mournful, like a mother calling in anguish for her long lost children, but blended with a pallor of hope and wonder, as though God were cradling them in His hands. Chris squeezed tears from his eyes and swallowed the lump in his throat. He sucked cold air into his trembling lungs and pushed it into the shelter with a whoosh. He grit his teeth, stared into the blackness, the danger, the unknown, and pulled strength from the music.

They lay on their backs listening to the haunting songs until light pushed through the pine tree boughs angled above their heads.

All went quiet.

Chris shivered. His head and arms poking outside his sleeping bag felt like a dog's nose. Tree roots and rocks pushed through the ground and tormented his muscles. He ran his hand over the bruise on his skull, his sprained thumb, torn fingernails, blisters, burns, and cuts. He longed for a hot bath, a warm bed, and a reassuring hug from his mother and father.

"Time, Chris?"

"Six. Sun's coming out. Let's get out of here."

"It's all downhill. If we leave now we should be in town by noon," Michael said.

They wrestled off their sleeping bags and jammed their feet into runners soaked with ice cold sweat.

"Goh! It's cold!" Michael blurted while rubbing his arms.

"Just wait," Chris said.

Chris pushed out the backpacks. Frosty air flooded the shelter. Clouds of condensation formed from their breath curled up and vanished into the pine boughs. Chris hesitated, sighed, and crawled out.

The dark lake, as still as a sheet of glass, was coated in a swirling mist.

Chris grabbed his stomach and doubled over in pain. He grabbed two bottles of ice-cold water, tossed one to Michael, and downed the other. His stomach knotted. "Wants food I guess," Chris said.

They packed up camp and left without a word. Chris looked back at the lean-to. He would miss this place; it touched him in a way he would never forget.

Four hours of non-stop pounding down the rocky trail took its toll. Pain, like a knife blade, stabbed through Chris' knees with each bone-crunching step. He ignored the danger of falls and twisted ankles and hiked at a near run, pulled down the mountain by the force of gravity and his determination to reach the island while their parents were still alive.

He glanced back. Michael was five feet behind him, looking down at his feet. Humbled by the morning's events at Natalia, Chris pulled his thoughts inward, not sharing a word with Michael. Chris tried to remember the terrain they had covered that morning, but realized he hadn't really looked. Only the waterfall remained trapped in his memory. It raged out of a hole tunneled through a mountain cliff, fell over three-hundred feet, and hit with a thunderous roar.

The midday sun drilled onto his skull. Hot air burned his lungs.

He paid no attention.

The trail leveled out. Trees became dense, the forest floor dark. Chris bounded over a rock and down a rocky crest. He broke through the trees and burst into a clearing.

A young girl jumped out of a chair. Her blue eyes widened. Her golden hair flopped over her mouth. She screamed. A boy, about five years old, sat frozen in his chair beside her.

A german shepherd charged. Its jaws, large enough to crush a football, clapped as it barked, growled, and sprayed chunks of spittle. Its chain leash, coiled on the ground, whipped up and snapped taut, flipping the dog up and onto the ground with a thud. It yelped and surged toward them dragging the tent trailer with it.

A man jumped in front of the kids. A woman gasped and sprinted from her chair. It collapsed behind her. She grabbed a thin metal rod from the fire and held it out like a sword. A hot dog, incarcerated into the end of the rod, bounced in front of Chris' nose.

Chris watched the hot dog bounce six times and cracked a grin.

"Uh, sorry," Michael and Chris said in unison.

"We, uh, we...we're, uh, coming down from the, uh, a night in the woods. Sorry, we didn't mean to scare you," Michael said.

"Do you mind if we pass through?" Chris asked.

The man stood straight. "Sure, go ahead."

They inched by the fire, keeping a wide berth around the tent and dog. They shuffled alongside a green GMC Sierra half-ton truck and onto a ring road.

Chris looked back. The family stood, their heads twisted like owls, and stared.

CHAPTER 24

"Cool, we're in a campground," Michael said.

Pea gravel crunched under their runners. A Volkswagen Passat rushed by, kicking up a cloud of dust and pushing them into the ditch. They stopped and looked around.

The road was lined with camping stalls -- a spot of gravel allowing for a picnic table, a fire pit, a tent, and one vehicle. The stalls were separated by patches of Western Red Cedar trees towering one-hundred feet above their heads. The air was humid and thick with the smell of cedar.

They walked down the road and gawked into each campground.

Most parents were sipping a drink, playing with their kids, or talking. A group of children ahead played a game of soccer. They stopped, stared, and whispered as Michael and Chris walked by. Michael waved and grinned at a little girl about four years of age. She burst into tears and ran to her campsite.

"What's the matter, Chris? Do we look that bad?"

"Wait till we find a mirror," Chris replied.

Although surrounded by people, Chris felt lonely, as though he and Michael were the last of their kind remaining on earth.

"Michael, a store and showers!" Chris exclaimed, pointing to a cluster of log cabins down the road.

Chris broke into a run. He grinned. Michael's steps receded behind him. He reached the buildings, charged into the laundry room, and leaned against a dryer.

Michael burst in and leaned over, placing his elbows on his knees.

He grimaced and panted.

Chris raised his hands up like he was praising God. "Washers and dryers! Perfect!"

"Something Katherine would say, Chris."

Chris ignored the dis. "Get into your swimming trunks. We'll wash our clothes and have a shower."

They dashed toward the men's washroom and burst through a wooden door. The room was lined with cedar wood. Chris counted four shower stalls to his left and four to his right, each with its own cedar door. In front of him was a row of sinks and urinals. A bench ran along the wall behind him. Chris reached up and brushed drops of condensation off the low ceiling. Like a sauna, the water and wood were warm to the touch.

They tossed their backpacks onto the bench, dug out their swimming trunks, stripped down, and pulled them on. Chris tossed Michael his clothes and grabbed his own. They walked to the laundry room. Chris slid four quarters into a dispensing machine and retrieved a box of Tide. Michael tossed the clothes into a battered orange washing machine and punched in four quarters as Chris sprinkled in the soap.

They raced to the showers.

"Chris! We have to pay for a shower!"

"How much?"

"Don't know. Says to push quarters into the slot."

"No problem. I've got lots. Here, I bought some soap and shampoo as well."

Chris jumped into his shower stall, stripped down, and pushed in a quarter. A blood-curdling scream filled the room.

"Michael?" Chris streaked out and burst into Michael's shower stall. "What?"

"My face?"

"I know, I've been living it for the past two days."

"They were staring at me."

"Uh-huh, I didn't know how to break it to you."

"Teeth marks! I look like a pin cushion! A black eye and, and the bruise on my neck, it's purple! Why didn't you tell me I still had puke in my hair?"

"Kraft Dinner? The bear probably hates KD after you puked it into him. I figured having some on you would keep him away."

"Hurry up, we stink," Chris said. He turned and opened the stall door to a boy about fourteen years old. The boy stared at Chris' naked form, then glanced at Michael.

"That's sick," he muttered and popped into a shower stall, slamming the door behind him.

Chris cranked the hot water until it burned. He washed his hair, coaxing lather from the shampoo on the third try. Scabs fell from his legs and arms, twirled around the shower floor, and vanished down the drain. His muscles relaxed. His thumb throbbed. He closed his eyes and rocked.

"Shut 'er down, Michael. We need quarters to dry the clothes."

They slipped on their bathing suits, pushed their clothes into the dryer, and dashed outside. Michael grabbed the laptop and plugged it into a receptacle. Chris lay on a rock, closed his eyes, and smiled.

The dryer buzzer rammed into Chris' dream. He snapped awake and shoved Michael off the rock.

"What the?" Michael yelled.

"Clothes are dry. Let's find food."

They sauntered over a graveled parking lot toward the camp office.

"What a dump," Michael said.

The office was the size of their garage. It was covered in grey, cracked siding. The roof shingles, cedar, were curled and covered in moss. Some were lying on the ground. A wasp flew to a rotted board under the eaves and burrowed into it. Chris grabbed the glass door and grunted as he pulled it open. A cow bell tied to a string panged. He tripped over the sill onto a wood-planked floor. Shelves packed with camping gear, fishing supplies, and food crammed the aisles of the tiny room. The walls were lined with pine wood. It smelled like popcorn.

Michael pointed to a moose head mounted at the ceiling. "Look, someone got your buddy."

Michael shoved Chris aside and grabbed a bag of nachos. Chris dashed by the sandwiches and snatched a package of powdered cake donuts and a carton of milk. Giggling, they staggered to the counter.

The lady behind the counter looked old. Her hair was black and thin, revealing patches of scalp. She had a mustache, a mole on her chin with a fat grey hair growing out of it, and was plump and short. Her skin looked like crumpled rice paper. Her teeth and fingers were stained brown.

She labored up from a green vinyl chair and limped to the cash register, puffing and wheezing.

Michael leaned to Chris' ear. "Will she make it?"

The counter lady rang the items into a dirty cash register.

"That'll be $11.92 boys, with tax."

She talked like her throat was packed with marbles.

She looked up, grabbed the twenty dollar bill from Chris, glanced at the items on the counter, and froze.

She volleyed her blue eyes between Michael and Chris, spread her lips wide, bared her brown teeth, and attempted to smile. "Where are you boys from? I ain't seen you around."

Chris hesitated. Why did she care? "Camping in the mountains, with our parents."

"Outside the campground? Where?"

"Natalia Lake."

"Beautiful, isn't it?" the counter lady asked. She curled her words into a sneer. She wasn't interested in the beauty of the lake, and Chris knew it.

Michael glanced at the floor. "Nice moose up there."

She drew her eyes to slits and looked at him. "Huh?"

Chris put out his hand. "Can we have our change please?"

"Yeah, sure."

The counter lady punched the keys, removed the change, and passed it to Chris. She bobbed and weaved as though she just discovered oxygen. Chris grabbed the change and rushed out the door. Michael followed.

Chris looked back. The lady had vanished.

Michael scurried up beside him. "What was that old bat so uppity about?"

"Dunno. Maybe she was happy to see ten dollars, enough for a pack of cigs."

"I think she saw a couple more trophies for her wall."

Chris tore open the donuts and shoved one into his face. Powdered sugar blew through his nose. The dough expanded and sopped up the saliva streaming into his mouth. Food had never tasted this good. He popped open the milk and gulped it down. It was freezing.

"Chris!"

Chris tried to talk through his donuts. "Whaff?"

"You're on the carton!"

Chris swallowed. "What the heck are you talking about, Michael. I'm just about in the carton, not on it."

"No, Chris! We're both on it. Look!"

Chris glared at Michael and turned the carton. "Oh, you meant it. That's why she was staring at us."

"We're on a milk carton, we're on a milk carton." Michael sang.

"Shut up, Michael. Not funny! Some kids are never found. We have to get outta here fast."

They threw on their packs and charged toward the exit lane. Chris looked back at the store. The counter lady stood at the door with her arms crossed, watching them.

Michael trotted faster. "Quick, Chris. Let her think we're leaving. We can double back and watch."

They heard the door bang open.

"Booeeeyys," the counter lady said, like she was talking through a glass of curdled milk.

"My God, Michael, she sounds like a disturbed goat."

"Uh-huh!"

"I have hot dogs and ice cream. You can have some if you want!"

Michael glanced at Chris and grimaced. "Probably cooked in a cauldron.

"Do you have any toads to go with that?" he yelled.

"Michael! Don't be rude!"

Chris broke into a trot.

They walked around a curve in the road and broke into a run. Chris pulled ahead, cut to the right, stumbled through a roadside ditch, and plowed into the forest, jumping fallen logs and ducking branches like a deer evading a pack of wolves. He circled and crept back toward the store, diving behind the protective cover of a fallen tree. He shook with excitement. He felt like a spy behind enemy lines.

Michael pawed at the spider webs plastering his face and hair. "Yuck! I hate spiders!"

"I've heard. Shusshh, I hear a car."

Like popcorn hitting the top of a cooker, the sound of gravel escaping tire treads approached from down the road. A police car appeared and skidded to a stop in front of the store. The counter lady bounced out the door, drew from a cigarette, and started to jabber even before the officer had left the car. "Is there a reward?"

The officer flipped open a notebook and approached her.

"Jabba the Hut," Michael whispered. "I bet she has Princess Lea chained up back there."

Chris grinned and stood. "Nope, probably mounted on her wall. Let's go."

They crawled into the forest and vanished.

Chris pushed through the Mountain Wood-ferns. The lush plants engulfed the ditch running alongside the road, obscuring them from the cars driving by. He led Michael at a dead run, discarding concern for the rocks and gopher holes littering the ditch, for they had to get out before the police car drove by. A stitch pierced his right side. He clenched his fist and pushed on. He could hear Michael panting behind him. He jumped into a clump of ferns and burst through the other side. "Oh!"

Chris stared at a cement plant and half a dozen warehouses the size of football fields. He'd never seen such massive buildings before. Beyond the warehouses lay a vast residential area. He stood on a clean, paved, and curbed road. The asphalt was soft. Heat waves rose from the black surface, contorting the buildings below. The odor of tar shoved the mountain flowers from his senses.

"That was rude," Michael said, appearing beside him.

Chris glanced at him. "What?"

"The asphalt." Michael wrinkled his nose. "Smells."

Chris glanced at the forest behind. "Coruntan. We made it. Stick out like goths in church, though."

Michael looked at him and raised his right eyebrow. "Goths in church? Are you kidding me?"

Chris grinned. "Works, doesn't it?"

Michael started to walk down the hill. "Let's sneak through the alleyways. The rail line is north and west of us. We just have to zig-zag through them."

"At least Kuma doesn't know we're here," Chris said.

"What if we meet up with the cop?" Michael asked.

"We'd better run. Let's go!"

They raced down the hill, through the industrial area, and ducked into a paved alley. The alley was enclosed with houses, most finished in vinyl siding and graced with lush grass, maple trees, and picket fences. Each had a two car garage, all with identical doors. Kids laughed and screamed from behind backyard fences.

We've been walking forever, Chris thought. His T-shirt, underwear, and hair were drenched. Sweat poured down his face, hanging onto and tickling his nose before a suicidal plummet to the hot pavement under his feet. Each drop sizzled as it hit the ground, seared by the heat and transformed into a tiny trail of salt.

The bruise on Chris' head thumped and triggered waves of pain through his skull. Stinging sweat invaded his eyes, multiplying his discomfort.

"Michael, I can't take much more of this. I need a rest."

"One more block, Chris. The street ahead looks busy. Maybe it has a store on it."

Chris dropped his head, shielded his eyes from the glaring sun, and counted his steps. "One, two, three, four..."

"...Sixty-two, sixty-three, sixty-four..."

"...One-forty-nine, one-fifty..."

"Chris! A 7-11!" Michael dashed into the street.

"Look out!" Chris yelled.

A silver BMW skidded and bumped into Michael. He jumped over the hood and continued as though nothing had happened.

"Idiot!" the driver yelled and sped away.

"Careful!" Chris snapped. He crossed the street, leaned against the brick storefront, and slid onto the sidewalk. He watched Michael walk in, placed his head in his hands, closed his eyes, and followed the lightning bolts streaking through his skull.

CHAPTER 25

A blast of cold sweet air slapped Michael. He shivered. Hmmm, donuts, he thought, inhaling the aroma.

Little kids packed the store, grabbing candy, chips, and pop by the handful. Half a dozen lined up at the slush machine along the far wall.

Michael pushed through the crowd and approached the clerk. Kinda' cute, he thought. Straw blonde hair, parted in the middle, fell straight past her shoulders. Her cheeks were freckled and her eyes, as deep as wells, dark brown. She smiled at Michael, drawing dimples in her cheeks.

She's not much older than Chris, he thought. Good, she won't be as sharp as that old bat at the campground.

"Excuse me. Do you sell subway tickets and maps?" Michael asked.

"You bet," she exclaimed. "Tickets are $2.00 and the map is free."

"Excellent! Can I please have two tickets, a map, and two large Slurpees; oh, and a bottle of Tylenol, please."

The girl pulled the tickets and map from under the counter, Tylenol from the display case behind her, and slapped them down. She punched $19.00 into the cash register. Michael gave her $20.00. She handed him the change.

She stared into Michael's eyes, drawing butterflies from his stomach. "You from around here?" she asked.

"Just passing through."

"Funny, I thought you were running from the police."

Vomit burst into Michael's mouth. He swallowed it. "Uh, what of it?"

"Just curious," she said, and smiled.

She looked really cute when she smiled.

Michael grabbed the tickets and dashed to the door.

"Hey!" the girl shouted.

Michael turned.

"What?"

"You forgot your Slurpees."

"Oh, right." Michael pushed to the back of the store and stood in line. He turned. The girl was serving the next customer.

"Think, Michael, think!" he whispered. *Should I run? Can I trust her?*

He glanced over the kids in front of him. A small girl about eight stood in front of the machine, frozen with indecision. Michael shuffled. Take the cherry.

He glanced at the clerk. She smiled at him. *Does she have a button under the counter? Yeah, no doubt. Wonder if she pressed it.*

The girl pushed her cup into the cherry dispenser. There were three more kids in front of him; more dithering. Michael's mouth dried. He had to pee. He stared through the front window, waiting for police cars to skid off the street, bounce over the curb and screech into the parking lot.

He looked to his left, the back of the store, at a door labeled employees only. If unlocked, he could dash through. It would lead to a loading dock.

He bounced on his toes. One more kid to go, he thought.

The boy stared at the root beer. It was empty. He turned toward the counter and screeched, "Hey, can you fill this thing up?"

"Take the cherry you disgusting little pig!" Michael yelled.

The boy turned and looked up. His mouth dropped.

"Look," Michael said, "I'll give you six bucks if you take the cherry, deal?"

The boy's lip quivered and his chin puckered.

"Look, I'm sorry, don't cry," Michael said.

The boy stepped back. "Sure," he said. "Give me the money."

Michael dug into his front pocket, pulled out a fiver and four quarters, and put it into the kid's stubby little hand.

The boy filled his cup and scurried out the door to his friends.

Michael grabbed two cups. They slipped from his shaking hands and bounced across the floor. The clerk looked and smiled again. He thrust them under two dispensers, not choosing a flavor. He stared through the window. Two police cars roared up, one skidding to block the front door and the other around the back to cover his escape route.

"Jeez, Michael, control your imagination."

He popped lids on the Slurpees and pushed through the mob. He stared at the door handle like a hunted rabbit.

"See ya!" the cashier called as he vanished through the exit. "I'll say hi to my parents for you when I get home tonight."

Michael shuffled to Chris, crushing the Slurpees against his chest.

"What?" Chris asked.

"No questions, here, take this." He handed Chris the Tylenol and a Slurpee. "Move! Now!"

"Pink lemonade?" Chris asked.

"Do you want a punch in the mouth?" Michael yelled.

Michael plunged into an alleyway north of the store. Chris ran up beside him.

"The clerk recognized me."

"Are you serious?"

"Yeah."

"Holy! They must have our pictures all over the place!"

"Quick. Let's find a place to hide," Michael said.

CHAPTER 26

Chris watched the Frisbee float over the grass. It scattered sunlight with every spin, and a black lab ran after it, jumping and trying to snatch it out of the air. It had been tossed by a boy wearing nothing but black swim trunks with pink skulls on them. The dog made a final lunge and missed. The Frisbee whacked the other kid in the head, because he was watching Michael and Chris so intently he didn't see it. Staring at Chris, the kid picked up the Frisbee and waved his friend to the road, where they walked, seemingly having an interesting discussion. The kids glanced back at Chris, rounded the playground, and disappeared. Chris popped open the Tylenol, dug out the cotton, poured a couple into his mouth, and swallowed them with his Slurpee. He stared at the fence, wondering why the kids seemed so interested in him.

Chris and Michael were crouched under a maple tree in a small park enclosed with backyard fences about five blocks from the store. Michael had the laptop booted up and popped open the wireless interface.

"Whatcha doin'?" Chris asked.

"Trying to piggy back onto someone's wireless. Lots aren't password protected. Just need to find one."

"How do you know if they're protected?"

Michael pointed at the screen. "Look here. That's a list of modems and their strength. The ones without the lock beside them are not secure."

"Holy! Six of them."

Michael selected a modem named Smart Guy. "Not very smart," Michael mumbled as he opened Internet Explorer.

"I'm going to type our names into Google news; holy! We're flippin' famous. Over two hundred hits. Here. This one is a local TV station."

Michael pulled up the news archive and clicked on a video file at the top of the list.

A reporter appeared. She was blonde, attractive, and wore a leather skirt.

"An update on those two lost boys from Silvertip. Apparently, they've been spotted in our city."

"So much for Kuma not knowing we're here," Michael muttered.

The reporter staggered up the camp road in her high heels as she talked and came to the store, to the counter lady who was bouncing on her toes just outside her front door.

"Uggh," Michael shuddered. "She doesn't fit the screen."

"They were right in my store," the counter lady proclaimed, flushed with pride. "I saw them myself."

"Did they look scared or hurt?" the reporter asked.

"They looked hungry and dangerous. The younger one was beat up, bruises all over his head and a black eye. It looked like a bear tried to eat him or something. Heh, that's funny."

The counter lady, seemingly pleased with her humor, talked faster. "The older one threatened me. He didn't want to pay. I stood him down, though. I think he had a gun."

"That liar!" Chris screamed.

"Don't worry, Chris. She's gonna explode in a second."

"Ssshhhh!"

"I called the police as soon as I recognized them," the lady continued.

"Did the police capture them?" the reporter asked.

"Dunno. They took off before the cop got here, cops are so slow. I tried to entrap the kids with hot dogs and ice cream; I figured any hungry kid would go for that, even a criminal. Not very bright, I guess. They wouldn't come back."

They switched to a police station. Half a dozen reporters quizzed a constable.

"That's the officer from the campground!" Michael said.

"Yeah, you're right."

"Constable, why are these children on the run?" a reporter asked.

"We're not in a position to speculate," the constable said with a military tone of voice.

"Have you apprehended them?"

"We haven't located Michael, Chris, or their parents. We implore all viewers, please keep an eye out for these children and call 911 if you spot them."

"Why would they not turn themselves in? Have they done anything wrong? Do they really have a gun? Are they dangerous?" a reporter asked.

"These children aren't dangerous and have done nothing wrong. I can't speculate on the gun. We don't know why they haven't turned to us for protection. I must add, Michael or Chris, if you see this, please call us at 911. Whoever you're running from, we'll protect you."

A familiar lump formed in Chris' throat.

Michael looked at him. "What's the matter?"

"So many people trying to help us and we're running."

"Should we call the police?"

"Yes, but no. I'm not giving up now. I'm sure Mom and Dad are on that island. The police can't get in without a search warrant."

"They just need a judge."

"Not with the information we have, a couple of kids, no way. If you want to stay here..."

"I'm going with you."

A screen door slammed in a yard behind them. Whispers drifted through the fence.

"Better get outta here," Chris said. He spread the map on the ground.

"Look. The train station is only eleven blocks away. Let's go."

They tossed their Slurpee cups into a garbage can and crept out of the park. Chris glanced back. Shadows paced behind a slat wooden fence like caged animals.

"Hurry. I think someone's after us."

Michael stopped. "Chris, if the 7-11 girl reported us the subway will be crawling with cops."

"Well, hopefully she didn't then. By the way, why was she on about her parents?"

"It was weird. She said she'd say hi to her parents." Michael trailed off. He jumped up. "That was a code! I bet she's given us a head start till her shift ends!"

"Could be, I bet it ends at 5:00," Chris said.

"It's 3:00 now."

"Let's go then."

CHAPTER 27

"See that path?" Michael asked, pointing to an opening between two fences.

"Uh-huh."

"I think it leads to the station."

"Oh."

Chris cut north and entered a paved trail. A fence constructed with rough-hewn lumber and painted military grey lined both sides of the trail and towered over their heads. He couldn't see the end because of a sharp curve up front. He slowed his pace and squeezed his fists. "Are you sure?"

"I think so," Michael said.

Maple trees spilled over the fence. They swayed, casting shadows like scurrying rats. Chris shivered. Though he welcomed the cool air it scared him. He moved to the middle, avoiding the smashed boards; the splinters, grime, and spit plastered over the fence like graffiti on an old brick wall. Broken glass crunched under their feet. Canadian thistle forced its prickly stems through the fence and stung his hands. He felt ridiculous doing so, but held them to his chest like a schoolgirl carrying her books.

Obscenity-laced rap music drifted through the boards.

"Careful," Michael whispered.

The path seemed to grow as they walked. Another curve appeared ahead.

The music got louder.

Chris leaned forward and peered around the curve. The fence

ended about six hundred feet ahead.

He felt like a pillow was held on his face. He had to get out of there. He sprinted towards the exit, breezed by two wooden pillars and skittered across an asphalt pad. He stopped and gasped.

Michael pulled up beside him. "Oh, Ssshhiuks," Michael said.

The train station looked like a war bunker. Eight metal doors, scarred and dented, were set into a blackened, cement block. Concrete walls funneled into them like a slaughterhouse drive corridor. It smelled of stale cigarettes, sweat, alcohol, and puke. It was a perfect trap.

Six teenagers leaned against the doors, smoked cigarettes, and watched. They wore old jeans, torn and dirty, and T-shirts that looked like they'd been washed in grease. Their hair was long and un-kept. Their eyes sparkled as though they had spotted a fancy toy to play with, or a car to steal.

One kicked a clean, yellow boom box. The music stopped.

Chris glanced around. A four-lane road ran behind the station. Beyond it, a Costco sign perched atop a building. The ground vibrated under his feet. An eighteen wheeler rumbled by. Could they run it without being hit? Probably not. Michael had been hit by a car already today. He wouldn't be so lucky a second time.

Chris turned and glanced behind him. He shuddered. The path was the only option. He tensed, ready to bolt. He caught Michael's eye and nodded back towards the path.

Michael pursed his lips and glared at Chris.

The teenagers spread out and blocked their path.

One of them flicked his cigarette onto the ground. "Where are you guys going?" he asked. Smoke streamed through his teeth. He was fairly small, had charcoal hair, and a hint of insanity in his brown eyes. He wore torn and dirty jeans, a black T-shirt, and a jean jacket with a snake on the sleeve.

"Mini motor bike gang wannabe," Michael whispered. He squared his shoulders and started toward the kid.

"What the heck are you doing?" Chris whispered. He glanced behind him and turned. Michael quickened his pace.

"Dammit!" Chris said. He sprinted after Michael.

Chris looked at Michael. Michael furrowed his brow, clenched his jaw, and glared at the leader. Chris scanned the kids. They were grinning. There was no way he and Michael could take on six of them. They were dead.

Two more steps to go.

The boy blinked and leaned onto his heels.

Michael shouted. "Get the hell out of our way, puke face! I don't have time for your stupid crap!" He pushed into the leader.

The boy stumbled and fell into the kid beside him.

Michael grabbed the door, pulled it open, and vanished inside. Chris dashed after him.

Chris' legs turned to rubber. He grabbed the metal rail. It was warm and sticky.

"Jeez, Michael, what drove you to do that?"

"Takes one to know one. Show them fear and they'll go after it."

"Fear? I just about peed myself."

"Yeah, but you didn't show it, did you?"

"Don't think so," Chris said, glancing into his crotch. "I was going to run back."

"That's what they wanted. Did you notice the abandoned garage?"

"Uh, no."

"Before we hit the path. It was trashed, falling down. It's their lair. I bet they've hauled a few kids in there."

"Oh."

They hopped down the worn cement staircase. About one hundred steps, it plunged into a dark cavern far underground.

The hair on the back of Chris' neck stood up. He turned and looked behind them. The kids were hurtling down the stairs.

"Hurry! They're after us!" Chris leapt three stairs at a time. The pounding of sneakers above increased in volume and intensity. "They're gaining!"

"You're dead!"

The words ping-ponged in Chris' head. He shuddered at the hatred.

Chris slammed into a red metal door and dashed into a concrete tomb. They stood on a platform bordered by train tracks sunk about five feet down to their left and right. Ahead, another set of stairs led out. He ran toward them.

A wave of air pressure hit. Chris ducked and covered his ears. A painful screech echoed through the station. A train, six silver cars shaped like torpedoes, lurched to a stop.

"Hurry, Chris," Michael yelled.

Eighteen sets of train doors slurped open. Chris dashed to the nearest set.

The gang broke through the metal doors with a bang, swinging chains, knives, and baseball bats.

"Where did they get those?" Chris yelled. He hit the train doors as they snapped shut.

"No!"

He shoved his arm through.

"Arrgghhh," he screamed as the rubber seal tore the hair off his arm, grit his teeth, and pried the doors apart. He paused, shocked at his own strength. Michael slammed into his back. Chris bounced into a metal pole and fell onto the floor. Michael fell onto him, pounding the air from his lungs.

Glass chunks blew into the car with a crash. A baseball bat flew through the window and cracked in half over a handrail.

"We'll get you, you little jerks!"

The train shot into the tunnel, pushing them to the floor.

"Whew!" Michael exclaimed.

"Get off me," Chris said. He gasped and groaned as Michael's weight left him. Heaving, he lay on the floor and watched Michael walk over the broken glass. It popped like Rice Krispies. Lifting himself, he dusted off his pants, walked down the aisle, and plopped into a seat beside Michael.

The train jostled, screeched, careened, and groaned. Warm air gushed through the broken windows. A fluorescent light perched above their heads blinked and pulsed, creating a strobe effect that made them sick.

"We escaped the gang, Michael, but I don't think we'll live through a train wreck."

A lady and a girl hopped on at the next stop. They gawked at the broken window and stared at Michael and Chris. The lady pushed the girl back out the door. It slammed behind them.

An old man limped in at the next stop. He wore dirty jeans with holes in the knees, a torn flannel shirt, and a baseball cap. His hair was matted and dirty.

Does he have a place to live? Chris wondered. He studied the man, looking for clues in his leathery skin. His eyes were dark and small. He looked down but, with his head turned, he watched them through his hair, Chris guessed.

"Six stations to go, Chris."

The train roared out of the tunnel and into a station, its floors, ceiling, and walls covered with glistening, yellow tiles. Chris guessed about five hundred people, their backs turned to him, waited for a train out.

Michael started singing Yellow Submarine.

Chris spotted a man wearing a black trench coat looking through their windows.

They locked eyes as the doors shut. Chris' heart jumped. The man opened and closed his mouth. He stepped forward as though to run to the train, but hesitated. As the train propelled away, the man fumbled through his left pocket. His right arm was held captive by a bulky green cast. His eyes never left Chris.

"Sheesh, Chris, what's the matter? Your leg's bouncing like someone's rubbing your tummy."

"I think we're in trouble."

"What?"

"I think I saw Joe."

"Shoot! Did he see you?"

"Yep, I think he's phoning ahead. He looks pissed. I think we broke his arm."

"Good! He deserved it."

Chris looked up at the map. "The next stop is Central Station. It'll be busy. If I remember right, it's only about fifteen blocks from the ocean. Should we get off there?"

Michael glanced at the ceiling and frowned. "Yeah, let's do that. We should leave the packs behind. They stick out like snow at a global warming seminar."

"Hah! Good one," Chris said.

Michael placed the laptop into the gidgit bag. Chris slipped their last $200 into his pocket. He placed the matches into the first aid kit and strapped it around his waist.

"Put your sweater on, Michael. It'll get cold tonight. I don't know where we'll be sleeping."

Michael grabbed the rope and slung it over his head.

"Hey, bud," Michael yelled to the old man.

The man looked over without raising his head. He smiled, revealing a few brown teeth and bleeding gums. In spite of his situation, he had a comical glint in his eyes as though he held a secret.

"Would you like a couple of sleeping bags and a backpack? We don't need them anymore and we're leaving them here."

"Gettin' cold at night," the man said.

"Middle door, Chris. Then we'll have the two side doors to run to."

"Take care of yourself," Michael said cheerfully as he dropped the backpacks off.

"Watch out for them in black. They're waiting for you," the man whispered.

Chris' heart leapt. He gaped at Michael.

Michael stared back with his tonsils. "I think we met the Oracle."

The train screeched like a swarm of bats and lurched to a stop. Chris grabbed a pole as he stumbled forward, and Michael tripped into him. The doors slammed open.

"Can you see anything, Chris?"

"Heads and hats."

Chris pushed into a crush of people. The air was thick with sweat and perfume. He felt Michael grab his sweater.

"Kuma could be standing beside us and I wouldn't see him!" Chris yelled.

"Keep going, Chris! Get out of here."

"Excuse me," Chris said. He pushed by a man in a pink sweater and dashed to an opening on his right. He stopped. *Where now?*

Chris heard a scream. He swung around. "What the...?"

Michael stood over a man in a trench coat. The man writhed across the floor like a snake with a heart attack. Michael held a black object. Two slinky wires from it were buried into the man's chest.

A gun dropped from the man's coat and cracked onto the tile floor.

Michael yelled, "Look out, he's got a gun!"

Pandemonium hit. People scattered, screaming and yelling. Chris pushed through the crowd. He reached Michael, grabbed him by the arm, and pulled him back. The object dropped from Michael's hand.

Chris pushed into the melee, dragging Michael with him.

"What the heck happened?" Chris said as they dashed toward the stairs.

"One of Kuma's guys," Michael said. "He grabbed me and pulled me away."

"And that thing in your hand?"

"Taser," Michael yelled back.

"Where the hell did you get a Taser, Michael?"

"I made it last year."

"Michael, you scare me."

There were two sets of stairs, one for leaving, one for entering, and an escalator sandwiched between. The escalator was still.

Like bulls on a run, a space encircled them. People screamed and dashed away. Chris glanced at Michael, confused. They bolted up the stairs.

Chris spotted Kuma and Joe barreling down the other side, pushing people in their wake. Chris grabbed Michael's arm and ducked.

"Stay down," Chris whispered while pointing above his head. "Kuma." He started to count. He reached twenty and yelled, "Go!" He popped up and froze. Whups, he thought.

Kuma stared right at him.

"Run!" Chris yelled.

Kuma and Joe jumped into the escalator. Chris dashed by them. Looking up, he couldn't see the top. He ran harder. He wanted to look back, to see where Michael was, but couldn't. A stitch cut through his side. His legs were numb. He heaved but couldn't draw in enough air. He stopped and panted.

"What are you doing?" Michael yelled.

A flood of police officers broke over the platform above like a wave of blue water breeching a dam. They split into two streams and flowed down both sides of the staircase. Chris ran into them.

Michael yelled and pointed down the stairs, "They've got guns! There's a whole bunch of them!"

They pushed through the station doors into piercing sunlight. Hot air hit them like an overstuffed pillow.

"Slow down, Michael. We'll attract attention."

People poured from the station, screaming and yelling, blocking the sidewalks and entrance doors. Police, fire, and ambulance sirens sounded in a fruitless attempt to clear vehicles from their path.

Chris grinned as he listened to the conversations around him.

"There were at least ten of them!"

"They had guns!"

"That kid. I think he killed that guy. Honestly, I saw him. He writhed on the ground in agony before he died!"

"He chased us up the stairs. I thought I was next. I think the kid's a psychopath!"

"I heard a loud bang! I think a bomb went off!"

"A bomb? Terrorists. For sure!"

"We've got to get out of here," Michael said.

A young lady in black stilettos, red leather mini-skirt, and white blouse jumped out of a cargo truck and bumped Michael. She shoved a microphone into Michael's face. Three men carrying cameras on their shoulders encircled them.

"Boys! What's happening? Did you see anything?"

Michael fell to his knees. "A huge monster, thirty feet high! Massive yellow teeth and red eyes. It's breaking apart the train like match sticks and eating the people inside!" Michael wailed at the top of his lungs. Tears streamed from his eyes. "Oh, the humanity!"

Chris grabbed Michael and pulled him through the camera men. They ran.

CHAPTER 28

Chris stopped and leaned into a wall. "Slow down. I've got a stitch." Lined with huge slabs of granite, the wall felt rough and cool to the touch. He wrapped his arms around his stomach and doubled over in pain.

"You're such a clown, Michael. Do you realize she's the reporter we saw on TV?"

"I know," Michael said. He gasped, giggled, tripped on a metal grate, fell to his knees, and howled with laughter.

Chris flopped onto the sidewalk. "Oh, the humanity!" he chortled. "That was a good one."

Michael squealed. Tears streamed down his cheeks. "The two most wanted boys in North America ran through about fifty cops."

Chris broke into a giggle fit. His abs spasmed. "Stop! You're killing me!"

"Can't, help, it," Michael said between giggles. "Did you see her face? The reporter? I think she just about peed herself."

"Michael, my gut's gonna split." Chris squealed and wheezed. He opened his eyes to a pair of orange DC's and white socks, and a pair of black Hushpuppies. He rubbed tears from his eyes and looked up. A young girl in a plaid skirt, her mother, wearing a green dress and standing beside her, gaped at them. The girl looked curious, the mother scared. Chris recognized them. They had boarded the train and hopped back off at the first stop.

"Get up, Michael. Let's go."

"Let's head north a couple of blocks, less crowded there,"

Michael said.

"Sure."

They pushed through waves of people streaming from the office towers.

"These buildings are huge!" Michael said.

Chris looked up. The glass, marble, and granite monoliths punched the sky. He stumbled with their sway.

"Look where you're going, kid," a man in a grey suit said.

Chris pressed into a building wall and let the man pass.

"Sorry," he mumbled. He stared into the bobbing heads. Although packed with people, it was a void. They were mindless and stoked with a common desire, to get out as quickly as possible. He felt small and abandoned.

"Yep. Some are over forty floors. The tallest building in Silvertip is twelve stories high," Chris said. "So, how do we get to the island?"

Michael frowned. "Rent kayaks?"

"Have you ever paddled a kayak before? Like standing on a soccer ball. We wouldn't stand a chance over a rough ocean."

"Okay, how 'bout a raft?" Michael mumbled.

"Hmmmm, I doubt it. That's a busy shipping channel. Ferries and barges use it all the time. We'd probably get smashed."

"We could steal a motor boat."

"No, I'm not going there. We're not stealing," Chris said.

"But we stole Jane and Greg's boat, and some money. I mean, what if it turns out they're on holidays and her brother runs a rabbit farm for target practice, or something."

"Thought crossed my mind, except for the rabbits. We know Jane and Greg and our lives are in danger. If we're wrong about this, I think they'd understand."

"We could work to pay off the damage we did to their boat and the money we took," Michael added.

"We'll never have enough money to pay for that boat," Chris said.

"Chris, look! McDonalds!"

Michael pointed to a small McDonalds set into the bottom floor of a classic sandstone building. It was ten stories high and capped with a curved rock banister. Gargoyles perched on each corner glared at the people below; a welcome sight.

Chris carried a tray loaded with Big Macs, fries, and hot apple pies.

Michael stumbled out of the washroom. Chris flopped at a table, popped open a carton, and stuffed the warm hamburger into his mouth.

"I figured you'd push the whole burger in there," Michael said.

"Hmpphhhm," Chris said.

Chris chewed until his jaw hurt. He swallowed and fired in a french fry.

"Michael, where did you learn how to build a Taser?"

"Internet," Michael mumbled through a mouthful of hamburger. He swallowed. "Did you know the word Taser originated from a book called *Tom Swift and His Electric Rifle*?"

"No, I didn't. Hmm, should have named them after Tom Swift and His Bludgeoning Hoe. Heh!"

"Very funny, Chris. They're actually simple devices, transformers, diodes, and a capacitor."

"Please don't tell me you tested it on someone's cat."

"Nope. I tested it on myself, just about killed me. I put it on my bum and pressed the button. The electric shock forced my fist to clench and I couldn't let go. I rolled around screaming for thirty seconds until the capacitor discharged. I lay there forever, paralyzed, before I could get up."

"Idiot."

"Yeah, but at least it worked."

Chris watched a group of teenage kids sitting at a table close to the window. They were whispering. One, a blonde haired girl with ponytails, pointed at Chris.

Chris stopped chewing. "Come on, Michael, people are staring at us." He guzzled the last of his coke, grabbed the rope, and hopped from his chair.

They dashed out of McDonalds and turned west. The buildings became smaller. Three blocks ahead a line of condos running north to south blocked their view.

"Michael. Can you smell that?"

"Yep. Sweet ocean air."

They ran.

"Look, Chris, between the buildings. It's blue."

They ran by the condos and up to a road following the shoreline. Only two lanes, the road was packed with vehicles. Chris grinned at the drivers, bobbing to their radios, sealed behind dark windows, and going nowhere.

The wind pushed through their sweaters. It felt good, but stunk like seaweed.

A beach, broken by an odd outcropping of barnacle covered rocks, lay across the street. Clouds of seagulls pierced the air with optimistic calls. Alive with white caps, the ocean didn't seem to end. Chris squinted. He couldn't see an island.

"We made it," Michael whispered.

"It's beautiful," Chris said.

"There you go. Talking like Katherine again."

Chris realized he hadn't thought about her all day.

The traffic lights turned red and the crosswalk light came on. The traffic was so backed up the cars were already stopped.

Chris and Michael crossed over to a sidewalk, down a cement staircase, and onto the beach.

"I'm tired," Chris said. He fell onto the sand and closed his eyes.

Michael plopped down beside him.

Chris' sweater drew water from the sand. It tickled his back. He opened his eyes and watched the clouds flow by. He looked at the waves tossing sand onto the beach only to pull it back again, a cat and mouse struggle between sand and water played out for a millennium. The sound calmed him. He dragged himself up and dusted the sand off. "Let's go."

They walked north, through driftwood, seaweed, and scuttling baby crabs. Chris longed to investigate, to be a kid. Another hour had passed. There was no time.

A man sauntered toward them. Sandy hair matched his shorts and leather sandals. A short sleeve shirt, unbuttoned, flapped in the wind, revealing six pack abs. He smiled as he approached.

"Can I help you mates?" he asked with an Australian accent.

"No thanks," Chris said.

"You lost?"

"Nope, we're fine, thank you," Chris said.

"Okay. Just checking."

"Looked nice," Michael said.

Chris glanced over his shoulder. The man watched them. He pulled out his cell phone and put it to his ear.

"He gives me the creeps, Michael. Let's go. There's something real big ahead."

They ran toward a grey shadow. It looked like a cloud lying across the beach. Chris could discern boulders as they drew near. They were tossed in a pile, rising from the sand and stretching into the ocean.

"I didn't know the Egyptians landed here," Michael said. He clambered to the top.

"Wow, Chris. You should see this."

Chris sprinted up.

The pile, about fifty feet in height, carved a line into the ocean, cut north, then curved back to the shore. A sixty foot gap broke the north length. A maze of wood floating piers, lined with boats, filled the inside.

"Wow, do you see that yacht?" Michael asked. He pointed to a massive schooner. It looked one hundred feet long, with a mast about as tall.

"What's that out there?" Chris asked, pointing to a blotch far into the ocean.

"That would be the island," Michael said.

"Oh." Chris' heart started to pound. "So close," he whispered.

"If only we could get our hands on one of those," Michael said, nodding toward the boats.

"Let's go. Maybe we can buy one for a hundred bucks."

They thumped along a pier and gazed at a boat bobbing beside them about thirty feet long and white. Four swivel chairs lined the back, each with seat belts and a bunch of nylon straps. A polished, wood lounge, bordered with smoke glass doors, rose from the centre. Above the lounge a loft housed a control room. Chris could see a sonar screen and computer beside the oak steering wheel.

A hand painted sign, *fishing for hire*, rested on the deck. A man sat on a wood chair beside it, drinking a beer. He wore cracked puma runners, blue cotton pants, and a red flannel shirt torn at the sleeve. His hair, curly and piled thick on his head, was as grey as the boulders. His skin, eroded by salt water and wind, was crevassed and thick. Tiny black eyes swallowed by puffy cheeks lit his face. He cracked a smile. His teeth, pearl white, broke from his grey beard and glistened with the boat.

"Lookin' to go fishin', boys? Heh."

"Sure, how much?" Michael asked.

"Three hundred."

"Sorry, don't have that much," Michael replied.

The man stood up from the chair. His knees cracked. "I'll dock thirty bucks if you don't drink the beer, heh?"

Chris beamed. "How much for a twenty minute ride, no fishing?"

"Hmmm, hundred. Where ya goin'?"

Chris pointed toward the island. "To the island out there."

The captain's wrinkles deepened. "Forget it. That's a private island. No trespassin'."

"We'll pay you," Chris said. "And you wouldn't be trespassing, we would."

The captain's eyes dulled. "What d'you want over there?"

"We'll give you one hundred and sixty dollars. That's all we have. No one'll know."

"Well," the captain drawled, "in that case, let's getter goin'."

"That was easy," Michael said as he hopped on.

Chris peered over the side. The waves ballooned as though pushed from the bottom of the ocean. Chris imagined a huge creature, like an octopus, with one large eye, swinging its arms like a wave machine.

The boat pitched and rolled under a fifteen foot swell. His meal balled in his stomach, erupted, and blew out of his mouth, splashing over the boat side and into the ocean. He burped up a mouthful of stomach acid. It burned his tonsils and felt putrid against his tongue.

Michael grabbed the railing beside Chris and looked over. "McPuke?"

"Hah hah," Chris said. He wiped his mouth with his forearm. He usually felt better after throwing up, but not this time.

The boat shuddered and pitched as the bow rose into the air. Chris wrapped his arm around the railing and pushed his feet out for balance. "Hold on, Michael. This is a big one." The boat shuddered and plummeted into a trough with a ka-whump. Salt water showered over their heads. Michael fell to his knees and hurled his dinner all over the deck.

"McFish food, Michael?"

"Shut up, Chris."

Chris glared at him. "Take it like a man."

Chris looked at the approaching island. It was bigger than he had expected. His stomach hurt, and his arms and legs started to shake. Nothing felt real until this point, and reality was cold, painful, and scary. For the first time in Chris' memory, Michael didn't scare him, because Michael looked small and frail against the rolling waves. The laughter in his eyes turned to fear and his boyish face looked brittle.

"You boys all right?" the captain yelled.

Chris staggered to the ladder and crawled up to the control centre. Michael popped up beside him.

"Landlubbers, eh? So, where do you boys want me to ditch you?"

"The rock cliff on the south side," Chris said.

"It'll be rough, but there's a sand bar in the middle. You'll get a little wet."

"No problem," Chris said.

They arrived in less than fifteen minutes. The captain pulled his boat up to the alcove.

"Jump in, boys!"

"Thanks, Captain. What's your name anyway?" Michael asked.

"Bob."

"Thanks, Bob, appreciate it."

"Be careful, boys. People disappear on that island."

"Now he tells us," Chris mumbled. He staggered to the back of the boat, climbed down a chrome ladder, and plunged into the ocean. Water surged up to his chest, and he squealed as the waves lifted him off the seabed. He bounced with them and flopped around, struggling to hold his balance with the gidgit bag held above his head. "C-c-c-cold, Michael."

Michael hopped in and squealed. A wave crashed over his head. He disappeared and popped up between swells.

They turned and pushed through the sandy bottom. Bob gunned the boat. Currents gripped Chris' legs, pulling him back toward the ocean. He tripped over a rock and came down on his knees, plunging his head under the water. He planted his right foot in the sand and tried to stand, but the current pushed him back to his knees. He needed to breathe but he had to hold the computer up at all costs. He imagined the octopus sea creature and felt something crawl up his legs. Arms tightened around his chest and he screamed, pushing the air from his lungs. He was yanked to his feet. He heaved, and realized that Michael had pulled him up. "Thanks, Michael."

They staggered onto the beach and looked up. The cliff was

vertical and crisscrossed with grassy ledges, many coated in bird poop, like icing drizzled over a cinnamon bun. The setting sun cast eerie shadows onto the crumbled rock face, carving the eyes, nose, and mouth of a sleeping giant.

The wind pushed through Chris' sodden clothes, chilling the ocean water. He shivered. "Let's go," he mumbled through chattering teeth. He picked a route through the ledges and started up.

CHAPTER 29

Chris jammed his toe into a narrow foothold, pushed up, and seized a clump of grass. It held. Pushing his feet into the cliff-side he dragged himself onto a plateau. He collapsed face-down in the dirt and panted, tired but relieved to be on top. Earth, grass, sage, and salt blended into an aroma that smelled like his dad's aftershave.

"Chris?" Michael called from below.

Chris groaned and crawled to the cliff edge. He looked down on Michael's head. One hundred feet below, the waves looked tiny. The island seemed to wobble, as though the ocean pushed it. "Don't look down," he warned.

Michael glanced between his feet, looked up, and glared. "Thanks."

Chris grabbed the rope from Michael and tossed it onto the ground beside him. He locked hands with Michael and pulled as Michael scrambled up.

The wind howled, pushing Chris back. He lay down and Michael plopped beside him. They stared up at a camera, mounted on top of a white pole cemented in the ground. It pointed inland.

"Perfect," Michael said. He jumped up, grabbed the gidgit bag, and pulled out a Phillips screwdriver. He removed the cover from a metal box at the base of the pole.

"Darn!" He slammed his hand against a red button inside.

"What?" Chris asked.

"A hidden intrusion alarm. I hope I caught it before the system did. Grab me a piece of electrical tape."

"What does it do?"

"It pops out when the cover is removed and sends an alarm. There's usually a delay programmed in. I hope I reset it before the timer ran out. If not, they'll be here in minutes."

Michael pasted a piece of tape over the switch.

Chris stood and peered through the dusk. They were perched on the edge of a massive plain, barren of trees and shrubs and carpeted in yellow grass. The grass reached Chris' waist. Swirling with the wind, it didn't look like individual stems, but a single organism.

Far in the distance, the field collided with a forest.

Black clouds rolled over the island and reached to the mainland like giant fingers.

The wind pummeled his ears, crushing all hope of hearing an approaching vehicle. Adrenaline boosted his heartbeat. His legs trembled. He tried to concentrate his thoughts, but fear tossed them around his skull like a ping pong ball.

"Chris, could you shine the flashlight on this?"

The cabinet jumped to life under the LED light. A black box was mounted inside, and connected to it a blue cable and a tiny, yellow cable. Chris recognized the blue cable from the computers at home.

"What's with the little cable?"

"Fibre Optic. The camera sends electrical pulses through the blue Ethernet cable. The black box converts this signal to light and sends it over the fibre optic cable to a computer. The computer converts the signal to video on a display. An operator can send a signal back to move the camera or zoom in on something."

"Cool. Whatcha doing?"

"I'm hacking the server so I can see through their cameras."

"Where does it end, Michael?"

"What?"

"You."

Michael grinned. "I doubt you'll ever find it Chris."

Michael pulled an Ethernet cable from the gidgit bag, connected one end to his laptop and the other to the black box. He booted up the computer. The monitor flickered, casting blue shadows over his face. Chris hopped onto his knees and peered through the grass. He listened to Michael's tapping against the keyboard.

Five minutes passed.

"Yes," Michael whispered.

Thumbnails appeared on the monitor, each a video stream.

"If I could only find a map of the camera locations," Michael said. "Ha! Got it!"

Michael pulled up a caricature of the island with blue dots showing the location of each camera. Each dot had a number beside it.

"Fifty of them," Michael said.

"Holy cow. There's no way we'll get into this place."

"Hold on to your shorts, Chris."

Michael superimposed the map over a satellite photo of the island. "Grabbed this from the Internet at Jane and Greg's house," he said. He erased the map, leaving the dots superimposed on the satellite photo, creating a near three dimensional view of the island and the cameras.

The island was about twenty miles long. The house, about two miles away, was nestled inside a forest.

"Must be that forest," Michael said, pointing at the spread of trees at the edge of the plain.

"Old growth," Chris said. "Those trees look as tall as the buildings downtown."

Michael looked up at him. "Trunks must be as wide as a house."

"Could you imagine owning this place?" Chris asked.

Michael frowned. "It'll never happen. How many rich scientists have you met?" He looked back at the screen.

"Look, there's a ravine to our right. It leads to the forest. Three cameras are placed on the west side of it. If we creep along the ravine under the cameras, we might stay out of view.

"Now, let's take a look."

Michael double clicked one of the dots. The front of the house appeared. A guard, armed with a machine gun, stood beside a polished cedar door. A white, plantation styled mansion, it had two stories and six pillars in front. There were fifteen large windows across the upper level.

Eight cameras surrounded the house. There were twelve more inside, most seeming to point at doors.

"This is interesting," Michael said. He clicked on a thumbnail. A room with a cot, sink, and toilet popped up. "Looks like a cell."

"Yeah, you're right."

Michael tapped the touch pad and scanned the room. It had no windows and only one door with a reinforced glass plate in the middle of it.

Chris' heart started to pound.

"There's four more," Michael said.

Michael selected the next camera and panned it toward the bed. "We were right."

Their father paced the room.

Chris' legs turned to rubber. He fell to his knees as a wave of emotion swept through him. He tried to yell, but tears weakened his voice. "I didn't want to be right, Michael! Dammit!"

Michael selected the next camera. Their mom sat on a cot. It looked like she was crying.

"She's wearing black," Michael whispered.

"So was Dad," Chris said. Tears blurred the picture on the screen. He rubbed his eyes and tried to swallow, but couldn't.

Jane sat on a cot in the fourth room, rocking.

Greg sat on a cot in the fifth room, his head in his hands, and stared into the floor.

"That jerk!" Michael yelled.

Rage pushed the fear from Chris' brain. Warmth swept his limbs. His skin prickled. He clenched his teeth. "I'll kill him," he whispered.

Michael selected camera-28 and panned around. A helicopter rested on a concrete pad in front of a large metal building. Two tanks, twelve feet in height, sat in a cleared area to the east of the building. A propane cylinder the size of a pickup truck lay beside the tanks.

"Bingo!" Michael exclaimed. "Fuel tanks."

"What about 'em?" Chris asked.

"We can blow them up."

Chris jumped up. "No! We'll kill ourselves! Look at how big they are. The propane tank might go, too. It'll obliterate everything!" Chris said.

"Got any better ideas, Chris? This will draw them out of the house. I've already seen eight security guards, all carrying Kalashnikov's."

"Kalishnikov?"

Michael looked up at him. "Submachine gun."

"Oh. So how do we blow up a fuel tank?" Chris asked.

"The rope is ninety feet long. We'll soak it with fuel, dip one end into the tank, lay it on the ground, and light the other end. We'll probably have twenty seconds to run."

"Not very long."

"We'll risk it. You heard Kuma. They're going to kill Mom and Dad tomorrow. And why are you worried? You're faster than I am."

"Not funny, Michael."

Kuma's voice blew out of the sky. "Guys. I'm coming back onto the boat. I think the kids are on the island."

"Kuma?" Chris exclaimed. He collapsed to the ground. "Get down. Where is he?"

"Relax, Chris. That came from my laptop. I patched into their radio system."

"Gord. Tighten up security," Kuma continued. "I want every man on patrol. If the brats are there, we can get rid of them once and for all."

"Will do, Kuma. We got an intrusion alarm by the south cliffs. Don't think they're smart enough to break into the security system."

"Get someone down there. These little pricks are smart enough to break into anything," Kuma said.

"I'll send a truck over."

Michael grinned. "Do you think he's mad?" He started to pound on the laptop keys.

"Better hurry. I'll direct this camera west and the ravine cameras up and forward. We'll run east to the ravine and follow it to the forest. If we stay on the right of the cameras and close to the ground we shouldn't be detected. Once in the trees we can go anywhere, unless we run into a guard, of course. We'll sneak to the fuel tanks, set up the rope, light it, and run into the forest. There's a small cinder block building in there. I think it's a pump house. We'll dive into the building and wait for the explosion. Then, we'll run to the house and into this door here."

Michael pointed to a door at the east side of the house. "We have about a thousand feet to get to the house. Once inside, we'll run downstairs and break them out."

Chris frowned. "What could go wrong?" He grabbed the tools and plopped them into the gidgit bag. The camera hummed and turned westward. Michael unplugged the laptop and screwed down the box cover.

Chris stood. A ferocious gale pushed him toward the cliff. He stumbled and fell. "The wind's swirling," he said.

He saw a flash of light. "Michael. Headlights. Run!"

The camera pole lit up. They ducked under the grass and ran. An engine roared behind them.

Chris tripped over a branch. "Ouff!" He hit the ground. Michael fell beside him.

"Can't see a thing!" Chris said.

"Stay left," Michael yelled. "Don't run over the cliff."

Michael jumped up and disappeared. Chris dashed after him. He could hear Michael's feet rustling ahead. Fear screamed into his head. Hurry! Hurry! He pushed himself harder.

"Ouff!" He ran into Michael and fell on top of him.

"Watch it, Chris!"

Chris jumped up and took off. He stumbled into the ravine, tumbled down, and thumped into a rock. "Ouch!"

Michael walloped into him.

"Let's go," Michael yelled. He slipped into darkness. Chris hunched over and followed Michael along the ravine edge.

"Michael, how can the cameras see us in the dark?"

"If you look up, you'll see two lenses. One is a camera and the other a heat detector. They probably have software that picks up movement, alarms the operator, and zooms onto the target. For all I know they could be following us now."

"Are you a cat burglar?" Chris asked.

"Nope, but I've stayed at a Holiday Inn Express."

Chris pressed his back into the Douglas Fir tree. The trunk was as wide as his bedroom wall and the bark thick with deep crevices. He looked up. The tree towered above his head and vanished into the night sky. Feeling dizzy he slid down onto his bum. "Let's rest a bit, Michael."

"Sure." Michael sat down and stared into the ground.

They were perched on a cliff above the ocean. The wind had stopped and the water was dead, as though waiting for something. Across the channel the skyscrapers looked like tiny doll houses, and a weird blue-white light rose behind the city and reflected into the water. "Nice," Chris said.

Michael looked up. His eyes were wet. Was he crying?

"Chris?"

"Uh-huh?"

Michael looked at the ground again. "I can see things," he said with a whisper.

Chris' heart jumped. He looked at Michael. "Huh?"

"I can see things."

"What? Like ghosts or something."

"Future. I can see the future."

Chris looked back into the ocean. Had Michael lost it? "What d'ya mean?"

"I have visions, dreams."

Chris shuffled and faced Michael. "Like what?"

"They're not clear. More like reading a poem. They don't really make sense until they happen." Michael looked up. His chin was trembling. "They always do."

"Like?"

"I knew someone would break into our house and something really bad would happen."

"Seriously?"

"Since I was four. That's why I made the hideout. Preparing."

"Four? How long have you had them?"

"As long as I remember. Since I was three. I've been scared."

"Of what you see?"

"When they come true."

Michael dropped his head. "Mom's dead, Chris."

Chris' heart clenched like a vice grip. "No! You're wrong. I don't care what you've seen. You're wrong. We saw her in the camera!"

"Maybe." Michael pushed himself onto his feet and looked into the forest. "Tough to hide."

Chris stood up. "If we meet a guard we're dead."

"Let's run from tree to tree,' Michael said. "One at a time. I'll take the lead. Follow me when I wave."

"Michael?"

Michael looked back at him. Tear stains ran down his cheeks. "What?"

"I'm sorry."

Michael dropped down, crawled under a fallen trunk, and dashed to a tree, throwing his body against it. He looked at Chris and waved him on.

Chris held his breath and dove after him.

Chris glanced at his watch. They had crept through the old growth forest for half an hour and crossed into a patch of younger trees crammed together and only sixty feet in height. He stepped forward. A branch cracked under his foot like a gunshot.

"Whataya doing?" Michael whispered.

Chris groaned. "Killing myself."

There's a camera," Michael said. He bounded over the forest floor like a deer and knelt at the base of a pole. Chris trundled after him. Michael connected his laptop and scanned the area. A guard stood by the helicopter. "Damn, risky enough without a guard," Michael said.

Michael disconnected the laptop and vanished into the trees.

"Where?" Chris whispered, dashing after him. "Michael?"

"Over here."

Chris discerned movement to his left. He ran, catching Michael's T-shirt as it vanished around a tree. He sighed and followed. Branches scratched his arms. He stumbled and fell, and crawled into a clearing.

Michael lay on the ground like a commando, staring at the tanks. The tanks were surrounded by a dirt berm, about three feet high and covered with weeds. The camera turned toward them.

Michael jumped up. "Hurry! Let's go!" He dashed to the berm and threw himself over. Chris glanced at the camera. It was almost at him. He sprinted to the berm and leapt over, landing in a patch of gravel and slamming onto his back. "Phuh! Oh God, that hurt!" He wheezed, trying to get his air back.

Michael crawled to the tank and sat up against it, beside a metal ladder leading to the top. "Come on, Chris!"

Chris felt a wave of nausea as fear and exertion sucked the life out of him. He looked toward Michael, but couldn't see his face in the shadow of the tank.

"Stay here and keep watch. I'll set up the rope," Michael said.

CHAPTER 30

Michael grabbed a ladder rung. It was slick and covered with black gunk. He darted up and peered over. The tank top was flat with a ring around the edge, like the top of a pop can. Rain water pooled inside and reflected the security lights' glare. His darkened face peered back to him from the water's surface. It looked wild with fear. The camera swung toward him. He ducked.

His heart pulsed inside his finger tips. He counted the beats. "…twenty-eight, twenty-nine, thirty." He peeked back up. The camera and the guard were heading in the opposite direction.

Michael grabbed the snap release on the tank hatch and lifted it. It popped with a loud clunk.

The guard turned and looked right at him. He froze.

The guard swung back and walked toward the helicopter.

Michael sighed. He tied the rope to the ladder, grabbed the hatch, and lifted. It screeched like a girl in a horror movie. The guard stopped and turned.

Michael froze.

The guard walked toward the tank. He had dark hair and a mustache. His ear glinted in the yard light. An earring? He wore black leather shoes. They crunched in the gravel as he hopped from the berm.

"We're dead," Michael said.

The man disappeared from view.

"Chris, look out!" Michael whispered.

"What?"

"A guard. Coming around the tank. I'll jump him."

Michael turned and coiled his knees. His heart pounded. He could hear the guard approaching.

Chris hunched against the tank. The guard appeared. Chris stood.

The man stopped and grabbed his gun, pointing the muzzle at Chris. "Who?"

Michael jumped. His knees struck the man's head, knocking the man to the ground. Michael collapsed and rolled.

"Get back!" Chris screamed.

Michael scrambled and looked back. Chris had the Kalishnikov barrel in his hands and above his head. He swung it onto the man's head with a sickening crunch. The man stiffened and fell limp.

"Chris?"

"I, I..."

"Jeez, Chris, I hope you didn't kill him."

Chris' mouth dropped. "I, I thought he was going to kill me."

"He was."

Chris dropped to the man's side. "He's still breathing," Chris said. "We better get him away from here."

"After I put the rope in," Michael said.

Michael dashed up the ladder and fed the rope into the tank. Gas fumes belched. He swooned, lost his balance, and slid down the ladder, landing with a thud.

He ran to Chris and the man. "I'll get his legs."

Chris pushed the man up and wrapped his hands around his chest. Michael grabbed his knees.

"One, two, three," Michael said.

They stood.

"Like a cooked piece of two hundred pound spaghetti," Michael said.

Chris staggered. "Guhh, how far?"

"Pump house."

They scrambled over the berm and crouched by the tank. The man was safely tucked into the pump house.

"How long?" Michael asked.

"Five more."

"Tell me when we reach ten."

Michael grabbed a stick and jammed it into the dirt, pushing it into a mound.

"Time?"

"Six minutes."

"Goh!"

The ocean waves crashed onto the shore somewhere beyond the trees. Michael started to count them.

He grabbed Chris' wrist and peered into his watch.

"Nine minutes," Chris said.

"The heck with it," Michael muttered.

Michael climbed the ladder, untied the rope, and pulled it out. Running down his arms and soaking his sweater, the jet fuel stung his skin. He left some rope dangling into the tank and secured it to the ladder.

"Let's go!" he commanded as he hit the ground.

Chris grabbed the gidgit bag. They scrambled over the berm and ran toward the forest. The rope grew taught as they reached the forest edge.

Michael lay the rope down. "Where're the matches?"

"Gottem'," Chris said. "I'll light it. You're soaked in gasoline."

"Sure, you get the fun part. Be careful. Fumes are everywhere. The whole place could go up." Michael ran for thirty steps and turned to watch.

Chris struck a match and walked to the rope.

"What if it doesn't light, Michael?"

"I'm sure it will."

A fireball engulfed Chris with a loud kuh-whump. A blast of hot air threw Michael onto his back, singed his face, and sucked the moisture from his eyes.

The fireball vaporized. Chris stood blackened and unmoving.

"C, Chris?"

Chris had no eyebrows. The hair on his head curled and smoked. Like Wile E. Coyote after a plan gone bad, he held the smoldering match upright in his fingers. His sweater was melted into his right arm. A blackened chunk of skin fell off, revealing a bloody mesh. His eyes bulged brilliant white against his charcoaled face.

"Chris, are you all right?" Michael whispered.

Chris fell to the ground. Fire raced down the rope like a snake on steroids. Michael ran to Chris, grabbed his arm, and pulled him up. Chris screamed.

"Move!" Michael shouted, pushing Chris toward the forest. "We've got to get to the pump house."

A blast of air pressure threw them to the ground. The area lit up like the sun crashed into the earth. Michael slapped his hands over his ears and screamed in pain.

"Chris?" *Where is he?*

Burning metal rained down. The trees erupted into flame. A chunk of steel crashed into the ground beside him. He jumped and bumped into Chris. The tank hatch screamed by their heads and slammed into a tree, slicing it in half. Michael threw himself onto Chris and pushed him to the ground as the tree fell onto his back. It felt like being hit with a baseball bat.

Another explosion struck. The ground vibrated. A chunk of hot metal slammed onto the fallen tree above them, lighting it like tinder. Flames blew thirty feet into the air.

"We've got to get out of here!" Michael screamed. He pushed Chris from the flames and crawled out. "Get up, Chris!"

Chris looked past him. His eyelids were half closed and eyes swirled around.

"Follow me!" Michael grabbed Chris' wrist, hauled him up, and pulled him to the east. He tripped, twisted his ankle, and fell to the ground. Ignoring the pain, he scrambled up and ran. They burst into a clearing. The helicopter, charred and dented, lay on its side. The Kalishnikov was wrapped around a propeller blade. The buildings and tanks had vanished. Fire engulfed the propane tank. A stream of propane hissed, shooting a fire tornado into the air.

People yelled from the house.

"Follow me, Chris. I think they're coming." Michael ducked into the old growth forest and ran.

CHAPTER 31

Chris crouched behind a tree and peered at the house. It looked like he was staring through the bottom of a Coke bottle. His arms felt like they were covered in stinging bees. He remembered nothing past lighting the match. He inhaled deeply and his lungs gurgled. *I'm drowning.*

"Michael, I think they've left."

"Are you sure?" Michael asked. He crawled up beside Chris.

"You, you've got blood in your ears," Chris said.

"So do you. Let's go."

Chris jumped up and ran. Michael blew by him, ran to the door, and grabbed the door handle.

"Chris! It's locked!"

Chris leaned on the house and panted. "Can't, freakin', breath."

An explosion, a noise bigger than Chris thought possible, threw a mushroom cloud fireball into the sky.

"Look out!" Michael screamed. He shoved Chris to the ground and dove on top of him. Windows blew in, pinecones and branches rained down, hitting the earth and bouncing as though on a trampoline. The house groaned like a sinking ship and swayed. Chris gaped. *I didn't know a house could move like that.*

"The propane tank!" Chris yelled.

A piece sliced into Chris' arm. He pushed Michael off and pulled it out.

Michael was on his hands and knees with three pieces of glass wedged in his back about the size of Chris' hand. Chris yanked them out. He pulled Michael up. Michael was crying. He yelled something, but his voice was muffled and Chris couldn't hear him.

"What?" Chris yelled.

"I didn't expect this," Michael yelled.

Michael's chin wobbled and tears carved rivers through the dirt on his face. He looked defeated.

No, Chris thought. We're not giving up! He grabbed Michael's shoulders and yelled, "we have a plan! Let's go!"

Chris vaulted through the window beside the door. "Look for the basement stairs," he yelled. They scattered over polished hardwood floors through the living room and into the kitchen. Chris ran to a door at the back wall and yanked it open. They peered down a dark staircase.

Chris jumped down the stairs and into a dark corridor. They ran to the end, turned left, and popped into a room. One wall was lined with green and orange vinyl chairs. An oak desk sat in the middle. A light with a metal cone shade, fed power from a long grey wire, hung over the desk and cast a dull glow around it. A comic book lay open on the desk; Batman, Chris noted.

A corridor to the left led to a room lined with white doors, each with a small window.

"Chris, we need keys."

They yanked drawers out of the desk and tossed them onto the tiled floor.

They heard a muffled boom. The house groaned.

"Michael. I found a gun!" Chris barked.

"Keep it."

"Got the keys," Chris said.

Chris ran to the second door, slid the key into the lock, and pulled it open. Their dad stared back at him, and his mouth dropped. "What the...Chris?"

"No time for questions," Chris yelled. He ran to next room and unlocked the door. His mom looked up and stared. Chris ran and gave her a hug. "I told you Michael! Come on Mom! Gotta get outta here!" He unlocked Greg's door, and then Jane's.

Their mom stared at Chris. "Oh my God, you're burnt. We have to get you to a hospital. How did you get here?"

"Later," Chris said. "Getting here was easy. We haven't figured out how to get back."

"Does your brother have a boat?" Geoff asked Jane.

"Yes," Chris said, "Kuma brought it back to the island after we landed. We saw it on the camera. It's docked northeast of here, about half a mile away."

"We should head there now," Geoff said, "before they know we're out."

"I think they're all at the landing pad," Chris said.

"What the heck was all the noise?" Jane asked.

"We blew up the fuel tanks," Chris replied.

"Are you nuts?" their dad asked. His voice cracked.

"Hey, it worked. Anyway, Michael's idea."

Chris passed the gun to his dad. "Here," he said, "you might need this."

Footsteps pounded down the stairs.

Chris crouched. "Look out!" he said.

Kuma slid around the corner, drew his pistol, pointed it at Michael, and pulled the trigger.

"Nooo!" Chris screamed.

Chris' dad pointed the gun at Kuma and fired three times. Kuma looked stunned. He stared at Chris, pointed his gun at him, and collapsed to the floor.

Chris turned to Michael. Michael stared down.

"What? How did she...?" Chris asked.

Their mom lay at Michael's feet, crumpled into a ball. Blood seeped from her stomach.

Michael dropped to his knees and pulled his mother onto his lap. He wailed. "Nooooo! Mom! Don't die! You can't die! Please. No!"

Chris threw himself beside her.

"Michael? Chris?" Her emerald eyes started to fade. She whispered with a tired voice, "I love you so much. I'm so sorry for everything. I wanted to be closer to you. I knew this day would come. I knew you'd have to find out. I didn't want to ruin it for you. I'm so sorry."

"What are you talking about, Mom?" Michael screamed. "Find out what?"

"I love you so much. I couldn't let you get close. I'm so sorry."

"Nooo! Mom! You can't do this! Come back."

She gasped and shuddered.

Their dad knelt beside them. He pulled Claire into his arms and hugged her. Chris felt Jane's arms around him. Greg grabbed Michael and pulled him close.

"What did she mean, Dad?" Chris asked between sobs. "What are we going to find out?"

"Later, guys, we have to get out of here."

"I'm not leaving her!" Michael screamed. "I'm not leaving!"

Helicopters roared outside. Machine guns crackled. Bullets thumped into the house. Chris closed his eyes. "Please hurry," he whispered.

She can't be dead, he thought. Not after all this. She just can't be.

Footsteps pounded down the stairs. Chris' dad cocked the gun and pointed it at the entrance. A police officer wearing an army helmet and bulletproof vest burst into the room. He raised his gun and pointed.

Jane screamed.

"Are you guys all right?" the officer asked, lowering his gun to the floor.

"You've got to save our mom!" Michael yelled. "She's been shot!"

The officer pulled out a radio. "I've got them! In the basement! We need a medic. Fast!"

Two officers thundered into the room, one carrying a green bag.

"Boys, you've got to let me work. Please, let her go."

"Come on, guys, let's get you to safety," the first officer said. He grabbed Chris' arm. Chris pulled away. "We can't leave her here!"

"Sshhh. It's all right, guys. She's in good hands. I promise you. Let's get you out of here."

Chris and Michael stepped away from their mother.

"Jane, Greg, can you stay with the boys? I'd like to be with her."

"Sure," Jane whispered.

A cocoon of officers surrounded them. Chris glanced back. The medic pushed down on his mother's chest.

"Defibrillator!" the medic yelled.

The officers ushered them down the corridor. Chris plodded in a daze, devoid of feelings or pain. He thought about one being led to an electric chair, his last day on earth. *Yeah, it would be like this.*

They marched up the stairs and through the front door.

Chris gasped. The forest was blackened and smoldering. A helicopter sat in the front yard. The propellers spun slowly. The whoosh-whoosh sound created a surreal and hypnotic effect.

"Wait here!" the officer yelled to the pilot.

They crawled into the helicopter and onto hard bench seats. Jane sat and pulled Michael close to her, wrapping her arms around him. His stare was vacant and his whole body shook. Chris felt Greg's arm around his shoulders. He rested his head on Greg's shoulder and started to cry.

The blades spun, and spun.

Their dad appeared at the door and walked toward them. Chris stared at his father, looking for a sign. He could see mourning in his dad's eyes. His dad shook his head ever so slightly at Greg as he entered the helicopter.

Please, oh God, Chris thought. Please wake me from this nightmare.

The chopper surged up and dashed over the ocean water. It rose high over the city. Chris stared down. The skyscrapers seemed so small.

They touched down at a hospital. Medical staff placed Chris and Michael onto gurneys and pushed them to the emergency room. People stared in hushed silence. Chris looked down. His clothing was burned and he was coated in a glistening layer of blood. Chunks of skin hung from his arms. He couldn't feel the pain. He couldn't feel his limbs, as though he looked at someone else's body.

The waiting room erupted into a thousand whispers.

CHAPTER 32

Chris stared into the light above his hospital bed. It pulsated like the pain streaking through his arms and legs. The bed was raised, propping his head up, which he was glad for, as his lungs seemed full of water and he felt like he would drown. He gurgled through an oxygen mask, with raspy Darth Vader breaths. He turned his head, and his skin felt crispy like burned parchment. He gritted his teeth and squeezed tears from his eyes.

Michael lay curled away from him. His body shuddered, and Chris was sure he was crying.

Chris sensed someone in the room. Looking toward the door, he found his dad, rings like storms under his reddened eyes, watching them.

Michael turned around. "Dad?"

"I'm so sorry, boys. We had no idea it would end like this."

"What's going on?" Chris asked.

"Chris, it's, it's not the right time."

Chris welled with anger. They risked their life to get here and their dad treated them like babies. He tore off his mask. "Yes, it is!"

Their dad glared for a moment and glanced at the floor.

"We need to know," Chris said, lowering his voice.

His dad looked up, past Chris at the wall behind him. His chin started to tremble and tears welled from his eyes. "Okay, I'll get Jane and Greg," he whispered and left the room.

Chris glanced at Michael, who gaped back.

Jane, Greg, and their dad shuffled into the room. Greg sat on

Michael's bed and their dad sat on Chris' bed. Jane stood between with her arms around her stomach. She stared into the wall as though trying to gather strength, then started to talk.

"My brother Robert is an evil man."

"My father was a multi-billionaire. When my father died, he left my brother to maintain the properties and businesses. Robert found he could access as much money as he wanted by paying himself a ridiculous wage and declaring everything else an estate expense. Over time he became addicted to the money, to the lifestyle."

Jane looked up at Chris. "My father left Greg and me some money as well. Not millions, but enough to live comfortably. I don't know why, but my father stated in his will that if I or my brother had a child older than sixteen years, that child would become the executer of the estate. She looked up at Chris. "The estate would then be divided amongst subsequent children as they hit the age of sixteen."

"That's weird."

"Yes, Michael. My dad always wanted grand kids, and maybe he thought this would encourage us to have them, even after he had died. My father didn't realize how cruel my brother would become. Although, who would? His lifestyle consumed him, became part of him. He was terrified of losing it.

"My brother visited us a year after our father died. He told us he would kill any children we had before they reached sixteen years of age. He knew we were trying to have children. He didn't know..." She looked down and covered her eyes. Her shoulders shuddered and she started crying.

"What?" Chris asked.

"That I was already pregnant."

Chris' stomach sunk. "No, you can't mean?"

"Yes, Chris. You and Michael are my children."

The room started to spin. Chris flopped back onto his pillow.

"I'm so sorry. There's no easy way to tell you. Claire and Geoff agreed to take you in as their own. It was the only way to keep you alive."

"Is that why you didn't want us becoming attached to you?" Chris asked his dad.

"Yes, Chris. Jane and Greg are your birth parents. We knew you'd find out by the time you reached your sixteenth birthday. We didn't want it to be hard on you."

"You and Mom will always be our parents," Chris whispered. "How could you?"

"I'm sorry, Chris. We love you. We felt it would be best for you."

Michael pounded his fists into his bed. "Well, you were wrong! My whole life is upside-down, and you caused it!" He burst into tears and started wailing. Jane ran to him and put her arms around him.

"Somehow, Robert got suspicious," their dad pushed on. "He sent Kuma to our house. Kuma tried to force us to admit that you and Chris were Jane and Greg's children. We refused. He got angry. I think he was going to kill us all when he sent his men after you. When you weren't in your room, it threw them off. They didn't know what to do. After some discussion, they decided to fly us to the island and wait for you to show up."

A doctor popped his head around the curtain. "Are you boys all right?"

Chris looked at him and said nothing.

The doctor cleared his throat and glanced at their dad. "Perhaps you guys should give them time to rest. We've got a room for them on the fourth floor. They're heading up in a few minutes."

Chris sat stiffly as his dad, Jane, and Greg gave him a hug. They left the room. Chris' eyes welled up and blurred. Michael wailed again. It seemed a million miles away. It all made so much sense. It felt wrong.

Chris woke with a start, popping open his eyes and squinting in the morning sunlight. He was confused until he remembered - they were moved to this room yesterday. The nurse injected something into Chris' IV to help him with the pain. He fell asleep almost immediately.

His head pounded, his ears screamed, and the burn was unbearable. An IV pumped cool liquid into his veins, which felt good. He clenched his teeth and hummed, hoping to distract himself, but with no success.

He pushed a button on the bed. A motor whirred and raised him to a sitting position. His hamstrings pulled taught and burned. He stopped the bed, fearing they'd tear. Even his chest ached from crying.

Michael was across from him, sleeping under a blue blanket and white sheet. The sun burst through a large window to his left and bathed the room in a warm glow.

The walls were green with an A&W orange stripe dividing the top and bottom. It looked kind of cool.

Chris groaned. The pain had to stop. He fumbled through the bed, looking for a call button.

A faint odor slammed his senses. He looked up.

Strawberries? "Katherine?" His voice was raspy like a draw file. He looked around, feeling panicked. Where was she?

"Katherine?" He tried to yell, but squeaked.

She appeared at the door. She looked like an angel.

"Oh, Chris," she whispered. "You're a mess. What happened to you guys?" She ran across the room and threw herself into his arms.

"Ouch!" he yelped.

Her warm tears ran down his neck.

"I was so worried about you," she said. "We saw the explosion on TV. They interrupted our show with a news report. I called the police. I told them you were on the island trying to rescue your parents, and they sent in a SWAT team."

"You saved our lives. They were coming down to kill us. The SWAT team stopped them."

"I'm so sorry about your mom."

"If only we had been more careful. We should have known that Kuma would come down those stairs."

"Chris. It wasn't your fault," Katherine interrupted. "You did more than anyone possibly could have."

"Not enough though." Chris heaved and swallowed the cry welling in his throat. "How did you get here?"

"The police flew us in. They asked us a bunch of questions. We told them all that we knew."

"How was the horse ride home?" Chris asked.

"Great, at least until we arrived."

"What happened?"

"Kuma was there." She looked away.

"Did he do anything to you guys? Is Thomas okay? Are your grandparents okay?"

"Don't worry. We're fine. He tried to get information about, about you and Michael. Grandma and Grandpa, of course, knew nothing. Thank goodness for that. I think Kuma would have seen through them if they tried to lie about it. He questioned us intently.

We pretended like we knew nothing, although we must have looked awfully scared. Grandpa got tired of it and asked him to leave. Eventually, he did."

"Thank God. I'm so sorry. The last thing I wanted was to drag you into this."

"It's all right, Chris. We're fine."

Thomas, Jane, Greg, and Chris' dad walked into the room.

"Hi, guys!" They blurted in unison. Their chirpy tone reeked of feigned happiness. Michael sat up. "Ouch! Oh man. I hurt!" he said. "Katherine, Thomas! What are you doing here?"

"Came to see you," Thomas said.

They pulled up chairs and sat down. Chris locked onto Michael's eyes. No. It wasn't a dream. Chris saw his mother lying on the ground. He burst into tears.

Damn, Chris thought, will this never end? How can I live with so much pain? He placed his face into his hands.

Chris felt his dad's arms around him. "Sshhhh," he whispered. "We'll get through this together."

They had stopped crying. Chris stared into a black speck on the wall. An anchor, it kept him from breaking down.

Their dad broke the silence. "Okay, guys, tell us how you got to the island and don't leave out anything."

Chris and Michael glanced at each other.

"Not even the kiss?" Michael asked.

"Don't you dare!" Katherine and Chris yelled in unison.

"Did you know Michael had our house rigged up with cameras?" Chris asked.

His dad looked at him and raised his eyebrows. "What?"

CHAPTER 33

"There's key chains, magnets, pads, and calculators at the door," Michael explained to the kids packed into the school gym. "They have a help line number, web site address, and text message number on them. Grab as many as you want and pass them around. If you need help, or anyone you know needs help, call the Kids Help Line. It's there twenty-four hours a day."

The school principal walked to the microphone. "On behalf of our school, I'd like to thank Michael, Thomas, Katherine, and Chris for their presentation today. As well, thank you for creating the Claire Boulton Foundation and setting up the help line. Check out the web site, volunteer, or call or text if you need help. Remember, as Michael said, kids will only be bullied if we allow it to happen. Let's protect everyone."

They left the stage to loud applause and proceeded to the gym floor to talk with the kids.

"That's four schools," Michael said. "Another eight and Silvertip is covered!"

"It's hard to believe we finally got here," Thomas added.

The past six months flashed through Michael's mind. He, Thomas, Chris, and Katherine set up the corporation, convinced twenty corporate sponsors to help them, and brought in over thirty volunteers. They opened a downtown office and hired a full time director.

Michael smiled at Thomas, the warmest, hardest working, and most caring person he'd ever met.

CHAPTER 34

Chris sat cross-legged in front of his mother's grave. Katherine sat beside him. A sunny spring morning, the snow had melted, birds were chasing each other through the trees, but there was a chill to the air. Winter was letting go of its grip on the landscape.

"Are you angry with her?" Katherine asked.

Chris squeezed her hand. "No. She and Dad did what they thought was right. She loved us, and so many times in my life I wondered if she really did. I feel terrible now that she's gone. I can't tell her I'm sorry." His chin trembled. A tear ran down his cheek. "I'm mostly disappointed. Mom was so much more than she showed and I never got to see it."

"How's it going with Jane and Greg?"

"Good, but strained. I'm glad we all live together now. Michael and I wouldn't leave Dad, even if Jane and Greg are our birth parents. It's different with them than before. Our roles have changed. I think we have to get used to it."

"Any word on Robert Cain?"

Chris stared into the treetops. Buds were starting, and in the sunlight he could see a faint green hew.

"Chris?"

"There's more, Katherine. Much more."

Katherine shuffled around and looked at him. "What do you mean?"

"I, I'm not supposed to tell anyone. I had a talk with Dad last night. Something didn't add up. I finally got him to admit it.

174

Katherine sat straight. "What?"

"Mom and Dad invented something. Something huge. Something so big they couldn't keep it secret. And it attracted Robert's attention. He tried to buy the company to acquire it, but the owners wouldn't sell. He tried to bribe Mom and Dad, and that's when he noticed us, and that our parents were so close to Jane and Greg. Michael and I became the biggest threat to him in the world. He needs money. Lots of it."

"What did they invent?" Katherine asked.

"Dad wouldn't tell. I begged him to. He said it would be too much for me to handle. He said it could change humanity."

"A weapon?"

"I asked him that. He said it could be used for the good of mankind, or control it, or destroy it."

Katherine shifted.

"Robert still wants it and he'll do anything to get it."

"Do you think he'll come after you?"

"Yes."

They sat and stared at the inscription on the head stone, feeling the breeze carry renewed life and energy through the trees, the grass, and the river. Chris pushed his thoughts aside. He didn't want to be angry right now, even at Robert Cain. He grinned, thinking about Michael. He'd come so far.

"Do you want to go riding?" Katherine asked.

"Yeah!"

They ran through the forest, across Jane and Greg's driveway, and to the newly built barn. Chris reached the door first. Katherine hit his back and pushed him through. They giggled and squealed, and crawled to the horses. Chris grabbed a blanket and saddle and tossed it onto the horse. He groaned as the straps slipped from his fingers, knowing Katherine would beat him. He slipped on the bridle as Katherine flew from the barn. He jumped on and charged out after her. She was just ahead. Her hair glinted red in the sun.

Chris surged into a gallop and chased after her, laughing. "You're not going to beat me this time!" he yelled.

###

ABOUT THE AUTHOR

Camping, hiking, fishing, hunting, and getting into trouble. What a great way to grow up. One of my favorite memories is sitting on the handlebars of my brother's bike, my dog on my lap, as he careened down the steep mountain trails above our home in Kamloops, BC. My brother and I had caves, tree forts, frog filled ponds, and cactus patches to play in, and sling shots for protection. Somehow I survived my childhood and proudly moved on to fatherhood. My children, Christopher, Michael, Thomas, and Katherine, kindly donated their names, characters, and ideas to the Boulton Quest series of books.

www.NDRichman.com

SELECTION FROM SINNERS, SURVIVORS AND SAINTS, SECOND IN THE BOULTON QUEST SERIES

Katherine envisioned six feet of earth above her. She felt ice cold water seep through the cracks in her coffin. She imagined bugs pushing through the loose soil. They would nibble through the wood, bury into her skin and lay their eggs. Fear raced through her cerebral cortex. Her cortex amplified the fear and rammed it into every nerve in her body. She screamed a piercing, guttural scream of mourning, terror, and hopelessness, as though a giant, flesh eating bug was dragging her to its lair, the last semblance of daylight fading as its trap door closed on her clawing fingers.

Made in the USA
Charleston, SC
31 December 2013